RED HOT BLACKTOP

DIDI POUNDER

A WORD ON TRIGGER WARNINGS

Do we really have to talk about sex and violence? Isn't that what sells? That's what they told me in... Never mind. This ain't about me, it's about *you*, and I owe it to you right up front to tell you that there's sex and violence in this book. Plenty of both. But here's a list of some of the other stuff that might trip you up. If you can swallow a little here and a little there, I imagine you'll have some real fun along the way.

- Sharp Levarius
Head of Trashcan Publishing

Violence, Physical Abuse, Suicide, Gore, Death, Attempted Sexual Assault, PTSD, Blasphemy, Foul Language, Late Stage Capitalism, and More...

ALSO FROM TRASCHAN PUBLISHING

- **CARTEL BOMBSHELL** by Didi Pounder - Lydia Slick, International Mistress of Danger Book 1
- **BOOKMARK FOR THE HEART** by Charlotte Northeast - Small Town Talk, Book 1
- **SABINE AND THE SILVER HAMMER** by Charlotte Northeast - Assisted Sinning, Book 1
- **DOWN FOR THE COUNT** by Ailis Elliot

Cover Art by Sean Peacock

@all.sorrows

Printed in the USA

First edition, 2025

ISBN - 978-1-968357-04-7

Dedicated to:
All the dirty sons of bitches
who said I'd never make it.
Suck it, assholes.

And also my parents, who are rad.

SNAPSHOT

Violet flattened herself against the rock face, feral terror beading up on her skin as she searched into the midnight desert. In almost thirty-six hours of freedom, she hadn't covered much ground. Sure, there was one way she could pick up speed and vanish into the night, but she'd be goddamned if she was going to give in to that.

Never again.

At least not if she had anything to say about it.

Her ears rang from straining through the silence. Even the dune crickets stopped singing, and she knew what that meant down to the marrow of her bones.

Things were about to get real fucking ugly, real fucking fast.

As if on cue, the night exploded around her. Deafening, ravenous roars chewed up the stars until she thought her ears would bleed. If it had started as a low hum, maybe she could have survived it. The kind of shit you read in romantic trash where ominous danger starts out almost benign.

But that's not how things work in the real world. It damn sure wasn't how The Pack operated.

Violet's heart shrank as the familiar, nasty, ripping pops of desert-rebuilt engines screamed at the sky. And, just behind that...

The howling.

The Pack was coming, alright. In literal beast mode.

"Fuck." The word tripped over her lips and fell headlong into the dirt as she ground herself even harder against the rocks. The raging motorcycles got closer, and she spat another, more deliberate, "Fuck."

Hiding was never going to last. Those sons of bitches could smell her, and that choked out any hope of laying low.

I'm gonna have to run.

Bolting straight out into the open like some dumb animal was out of the question. That would drop her right back in their clutches, and her whole escape gambit would have been for shit.

No, she needed a plan. Or, at least something like it.

Violet squeezed her eyes shut and bumped the back of her head against the boulder a few times, fighting to get her breath under control. Anything to make the world feel real again. The blare of The Pack spiked, and she snapped her eyes open to see the sickly glow of their headlights carving hunks out of the darkness.

Staring wildly across the horizon, she spotted a lifeline – a set of headlights idling down the dark desert highway.

A big rig truck.

In all her aimless scrambling, Violet had made it to the interstate.

No wonder The Pack was coming in hard and fast. She was almost free. If lady luck would look her way just once in her whole, miserable life, Violet would never have to see a single one of those mangy faces ever again.

"Here goes nothing."

Creeping low, she ducked behind some rubble and tried to gauge the distance. It was going to be one hell of a hard sprint. Maybe too hard.

A white hot finger of light cut through the gloom, reaching for Violet's back. Her heart swelled against her ribs so hard she thought they would crack. The deafening chorus of engines shredded up behind her, and before she knew it, she was running at top speed. The Pack was hot on her tail, but she had to make it to the road.

It's the highway or nothing.

ONE

Son of a bitch, I'm beat.

The fluorescent diner lights buzzed just enough to set Truck's teeth on edge. He looked down at the yellow smear of yolk and hash brown grease on his plate and scrunched his eyes shut.

It'd been one hell of a haul.

He would have murdered his own stepfather for another cup of coffee, but all that would do was keep him awake. That was the last thing he wanted.

No, what he really needed was to find a rest stop, climb in the back of his rig, and sleep for about twelve years. He'd ground out nearly eighteen hundred miles in a rat's hair under twenty four hours, and that's *with* stopping for gas. A push like that was a bona fide bastard, but bastards were his specialty.

That's why they hired him.

Everybody knew Tucker 'Truck' Laine could burn the candle at both ends and the middle.

"Take your time, sexy." The waitress dropped the check and gave him the kind of lingering once over that told him exactly where her head was at.

Did she knock open another button on her blouse?

The generous crease of cleavage said yes.

"Thanks." In spite of himself, he offered his patented come-hither smile, making no attempt to hide his appraisal of the goods she laid out on display. She was older than him, but Truck was never the kind of guy to worry over a woman's age. Not the good looking ones, anyway.

Besides, he'd be lying if he said he hadn't been stealing glances at her figure since he sat down. A bit too much eye shadow, but he had a soft spot for that kind of thing.

She sauntered off, and he turned in his booth to catch the extra dash of swing she threw into her hips. The lady had what his grandfather would have called, "One hell of a gripper."

Swiping up one last forkful, he got up and strolled to the line of coolers at the far end of the diner. If there's one thing he loved about the truck-stop lifestyle, it was the one-stop-shopping nature of it all. More coffee was out of the question, but Truck had other lullaby libations in mind. After all, he didn't have another load straight away, so nobody could say shit about how he spent the night.

Pulling two frosty tallboys out of the deep chill, Truck looked over his shoulder to see the smoky-eyed bottle blonde leaning over the cash register watching him like a lioness on a mountaintop. Should he play the gentleman and pull a cold one for her as well?

"Nah," he whispered to himself. "Not tonight."

If he hadn't just pushed like the devil to meet his drop, he'd gladly have coaxed her out to his rig and given her a night to remember. There was no way it would have been the first dome light she'd kicked her heels at, but if he had the energy, it'd be the one she told her grandkids about over some awkward Thanksgiving dinner.

Anything to break up the monotony of the road. Life behind the wheel could get pretty lonely. Especially out west where the CB radio didn't offer up much beyond static and bored retirees aching for someone to talk to besides their wives. The sound of their voices only made Truck feel more adrift, so he tended to keep the squawk box switched off when he was in this part of the world.

So, when it came to company, that only left the woman at the till. She'd seen more than her share of bad road, and had the sad-hungry eyes to prove it.

There was a kinship in high mileage lives like the ones they led, but Truck couldn't bring himself to lean into it. Sometimes it was better to be lonely by himself than to curl up next to another lost soul. By morning they'd both be hollowed out. Well fucked, sure, but empty where it really counts.

That said, he wasn't above helping himself to an eyeful as long as it was on offer. And boy howdy, this lady laid out the samples.

"Can I get some ID?" she purred when he stepped up to the counter and clapped down the already sweating cans.

"Sure." He pulled his license out with a smirk, handing it into a set of improbably long, pink nails.

Jesus Christ, woman, another button?

Her breasts were in serious danger of tumbling out where any old body could get an eyeful. There at the center of the canyon, just past the dime store gold cross, Truck could see the clasp of her front-fastening bra.

This lady means business.

"Tucker, huh?" She turned his license over in her fingers, lightly biting the tip of her tongue.

"That's right," he replied, keeping it cool.

"I bet you really know how to 'tuck her,' don't you?"

Brazen as shit, ain't she?

To say she was begging for it would have been an insult to the subtlety of beggars everywhere. Truck couldn't resist stirring her up.

"Never had any complaints." An extra glint in his eye

added just enough sauce to this well-worn exchange to make her knees visibly shudder.

"Well, *Tuck-her.*" She tapped a beer with a lacquered nail, keeping her gaze leveled on his. "Will this be all tonight? Or is there anything else you're looking to pick up?"

"I'm afraid this will be it for the evening." He slipped a twenty onto the counter, and their fingers brushed as he took back his ID. "I'd be a shame if someone were to come in to find the place empty. Don't want to get you in trouble."

"Oh, nobody comes this time of night."

"You and I both know that's not true," he said, voice as rich and lethal as a panther. "It'd be a shame if *nobody* came tonight."

Her eyes damn near popped. She stammered for a moment, and Truck gave a lazy sigh, picked up the beers, and glanced at the 2am clock on the wall with a raised eyebrow.

"Even so, I'd never forgive myself if I made you miss the breakfast rush." He leaned over the counter far enough to smell her lip gloss. She trembled as Truck took a long look at her front real estate, fetching her name off the tag. "I can tell you one thing, Heather."

"What's that?" Her lashes fluttered like she might fly away on them.

"You'd be one hell of a reason to miss breakfast." This time, her knees buckled in earnest. Truck chuckled as he headed for the door, turning back just long enough to glance over his shoulder. "By the way, my mom calls me Tucker. To everybody else, I'm Truck."

As the bell jangled behind him, Truck could almost swear he heard her faint dead on the chipped linoleum.

Climbing back into his chrome fronted castle, Truck snugged one of the beers into a koozie and slid it into the cup holder before tossing the other in the passenger seat. It was sorely tempting to go ahead and crack the can to treat himself, but he held back.

Best not, he thought. *Cops are always crawling on nights like this. Can't give 'em an excuse.*

Sighing and looking at the moisture beading up on the can, he doubled down on his decision to wait and turned the key. That glorious rumble rose up around him, fetching a weary smile.

"Come on, Layla." He patted the steering wheel with true affection. "Let's find a place to call it a night." Layla shifted into drive and rolled away from the glare of late night lights, straight onto two lanes of paved freedom.

A rest stop would have been nice, but at the moment all he wanted was a stretch of shoulder where the stars could twinkle through the windshield.

Steering out towards the heart of the desert, all he could think of was how good the couple of beers would taste when he climbed back into the sleeping compartment to sack out.

Coming around a cluster of boulders onto the straightaway, he saw headlights ahead. Not just a single car, either.

"What the hell?"

Letting up on the gas a bit, Truck squinted in disbelief. The lights fanned out across both lanes, spilling over onto the shoulder on either side. This wasn't some midnight traveler – this was a goddamn battalion.

"Motorcycles," he grumbled. "Shit. Only assholes ride motorcycles."

Easing down to a crawl, he tried to gauge just what this encounter was going to look like. Bikers had a reputation for being stone dickholes way out here in the sticks, and the last thing Truck wanted was a twenty five bike tail chasing him until sunup. Shaking a batch of rednecks with nothing better to do than crank their hogs wasn't on Truck's to-do list.

Straddling the center line, he gritted his teeth and hoped they'd part like the red sea and let him pull on through. Maybe he'd catch a lucky break.

"The fuck is that?"

Something right at the head of this shitshow seemed off, and he squinted even harder to try and make out what it was. When he did, his blood turned to iced tea.

At the very front of the glare was a silhouette. Running.

It would be one thing if a bunch of drunk fuckers had corralled some deer onto the asphalt, getting their jollies out of frightening the shit out of it before gunning it down. Shitty, but not unheard of. Trouble was, deer didn't run like that. Only one animal under the great big sky ran like that.

It was a person.

A woman.

Hurtling like hell right down the middle of the goddamn interstate.

Something in Truck's belly caught fire, and he was in no mood to put it out. This wasn't even a goddamn manhunt. This was pure torture for sport, and his throat went tight thinking what was waiting for this girl when those fuckers got tired of rattling their mufflers and flexing their dicks.

"You know what?" Even alone, Truck's voice came out like steel. "Fuck this."

Slamming into gear, he gripped the wheel like the prow of a chariot. Serious shit was about to go down, and he was here to party. Getting involved usually wasn't his thing, but tonight he was just going to have to make an exception.

TWO

Thank God!

Violet locked on the headlights and sprinted until her legs were ready to shatter under her. The Pack saw them too, and the roar of engines closing up behind her doubled in intensity. They'd been gobbling up the road, but now they threatened to swallow it whole – and her with it.

Her throat was all cold fire as she heaved in great lungfuls of midnight air. Careening towards the rig barreling straight at her, she waved her arms over her head, desperate to be seen against the glare on her heels.

"Hey," she screamed. "Help!"

The big rig slurped up the center line on a direct collision course with her tiny frame. Not that she cared. If the damned thing pasted her to the road, maybe it would save her from the ungodly levels of mayhem coming her way if The Pack scooped her up.

Maybe.

All at once, the truck veered to her left as if the driver had been asleep and only just saw some girl running up the middle of the road like a crazy person. It juddered past her, and her heart turned to ice.

He's gonna leave me here.

Eighteen wheels churned up a hurricane of dust as the driver skidded along the shoulder. Rubber squealed against the blacktop, and Violet watched as the rig banked hard across the road. It was a steep cut, and the mountain of truck slued and shook like it was gonna tip over and roll into a tangled wreck.

Putting up a hand to shield her mouth from the cloud of dirt, she stood in absolute wonder. The trailer stretched across both lanes, slicing an impenetrable line between Violet and the marauding band of fuckers at her heels. A chorus of screeching brakes sliced through the darkness as The Pack tried like hell to keep from slamming into the far side. The cacophony of squawling tires washed over her like a choir of angels from on high.

The door of the cab kicked open, and a hand shot out in her direction. "Come on!" With a few quick bounds, she caught the offered palm and an iron grip snatched her into the truck. She lay across this stranger's lap, panting with terror and exhaustion.

"Hang on," the man said, and jerked at the gear shift next to her head. The rig bucked like the devil's own bronco, damn near flinging her backwards through the still-open door. She clutched at the seat, and her savior released the gear shift to seize the wheel. That done, he reached down and clamped his other arm around her waist.

For an agonizing moment, the whole world seemed ready to split as the truck strained and lurched. Even without being told, Violet knew when the trailer pulled straight. In a flash, the truck surged forward like a greyhound after a mechanical rabbit. Her heels kicked through the open door, wind whistling around her bare legs.

"Ankles up."

"What?" She craned her neck to see if she had heard him right.

"Ankles up," he said again through clenched teeth,

attention locked on the road ahead. She bent her knees, and his hand unfurled from her waist and slammed the door. Wriggling over his lap, Violet dragged herself into the passenger seat and got her first good look at the man who yanked her out of the mouth of hell.

Maybe it was the salvation talking, but this guy was pretty goddamn hot. Like, built-like-something-out-of-Greek-mythology levels of hot. Broad chest, sleeves rolled above the elbow revealing python thick arms. This man was the picture book version of a working class Hercules.

Whatever he looked like, he was hero enough for her.

"You're gonna want to buckle up," he said, making eye contact with her for the first time.

"Why?"

"Because we might have to go off-road."

She swallowed hard, and pulled a frosty beer from behind the small of her back and jabbed it into a cup holder. The seatbelt fumbled like a fucker in her hands before finally clicking into place. It didn't help that the cab reared and plunged like a mechanical bull, but so be it. Even above the growl of his engine, she could hear the wild, chainsaw thunder of The Pack.

Turns out, "might have to" was a direct translation of, "we're doing this shit."

Violet super glued her face to the window, only to find a handful of choppers pacing them. Behind each headlight leered a hatefully familiar face, blistered with anger. Her bones shook under her skin thinking what would happen if they got her now.

Not that the dynamo in the driver's seat was gonna make it easy.

"How many?" His voice caught her off guard.

"What?"

"I've got seven on the left here, and can only see four over there. Anybody in my blind spot?"

Violet pressed her forehead to the glass.

"Five total. But there's more—"

"Yeah, I know," he cut her off. "There's more in the back." With that, he stomped hard on the gas. The truck ran high and loud before the transmission knuckled down to meet the push. "You mind if I sweep these fuckers?" He cut his eyes over to her, and Violet could almost swear he was enjoying this.

"Go for it." The words weren't even out before he snapped the wheel.

If she hadn't been wearing a seatbelt, she would have flown straight into his lap – which might not have been such a terrible fate. They jolted over the shoulder, and the cab rocked like a bomb had gone off. A sharp dip sent her stomach sailing up to her collarbone.

At that speed, even an eighteen wheeler jumps like the goddamn General Lee.

A terrible banging rasped up from the trailer as the riders too dumb to get out of the way got cleaned out. Violet ached to see who it was, and whether they had been knocked off their bikes. A Grapes of Wrath level dust bowl obscured the carnage, but she reveled in the likelihood of it.

In all the madness, they'd made short work of some poor schmuck's barbed wire fence and tore out onto open pasture. If there were any cows out there, they were gonna have to watch the fuck out.

The front corner of the cab clipped a massive saguaro cactus, and it exploded into pulp with about a billion bee stingers in the mix.

"Fuckin' right," the driver cheered. "Got 'em!"

"You did?"

"Yup. Pasted them with all that shit."

Clicking off her belt, Violet lunged across his lap to see the damage. A whole tangle of bikes guttered and spun away from them, the riders screaming and swearing almost as loud as their engines.

"Easy with that."

"What?" She pulled her eyes from the glass and her breath came in short to see how close she was to his face. He nodded down to his lap. Her hand was so high on his thigh, it was two stitches away from the danger zone.

"Sorry!" She scrambled back to her seat, flushed with more than the thrill of the chase.

"You're gonna want to get that belt back on," he said. "Last thing I want is to get you away from those guys only to have you get all banged up in here."

Getting banged up in here might not be so bad, she thought before she could catch herself.

It wasn't like her to get all spicy. Her blood must've really been up with all the danger and the rescue. Whatever it was, she cinched herself back into place.

To her shock, they started to slow down. Motorcycle engines bellowed in victory, and leather clad monsters began to swamp up either side of the rig.

"What are you doing?" Violet teetered on the verge of panic, but the driver just nodded ahead. About a hundred yards in front of them stood a billboard yelling about a purportedly famous roadside attraction at some gas station. It was gaudy as hell, and they were headed straight for it.

"Oh, fuck." Gripping her seat until her nails threatened to rip the fabric, she pushed back against the seat and braced for impact. The sickening yellow paint loomed larger and larger as they gained ground, but at the last second, the driver yanked the wheel to the left. They whizzed by the billboard so close it raked along the side of the trailer, scraping off members of The Pack into a weltering knot of metal and fury.

No sooner had they cleared the billboard than red and blue lights flashed up.

"Goddamnit," the driver muttered. Speed traps must ha

been the bane of his stock and trade, but as far as Violet was concerned this was divine intervention.

The trucker hit his emergency blinkers and shambled back towards the highway, a squad car following in their wake.

Choppers shot off in all directions, splintering out into the darkness. If there was one thing The Pack was pretty scrupulous about, it was keeping clear of the fuzz. Not that they were afraid of cops – they had no reason to be – but, given the rout they'd just been put through, there were wounds to be licked.

It was clear that this truck driver – whoever he was – was just about as formidable an opponent as they could find. That simple fact made her skin prickle, and she got all quivery in the pit of her stomach. That quiver turned into a full-on butterfly parade as they pulled to a stop next to the highway and the driver looked her full in the face.

His chestnut hair swept back over a pair of keen, startling eyes. The kind that had seen more than their fair share of shit. A surprisingly attractive Tom Selleck mustache hid his upper lip, but she could still read concern in every flicker of his face.

"Are you okay?" he asked.

"I think so," she replied, vibrating from the adrenaline sizzling in her veins. "Thank you."

Violet knew it would be a crime to drag anybody else into her situation, least of all this rugged champion.

Trouble was, she knew in her bones she was going to have one hell of a time letting him go.

THREE

"Alright, Mr. Laine, all your paperwork seems to be in order."

You're goddamn right it is, Truck smirked. He hated cops under the best of circumstances, and tonight's circumstances were shit. Sure, the boy in blue was something of a white knight, but he still had that special brand of smug entitlement that always sits on the other side of a badge.

"Thanks," Truck said, turning to hike himself back behind the wheel.

"Hang on." That telltale pen click slithered down Truck's spine like a copperhead. "I still have to cite you."

"For what?" It was a struggle to sound incredulous more than outright angry.

"Can't say you were speeding, necessarily, but there's destruction of property, invasion of private property..."

"I was being chased by a goddamn motorcycle gang, what was I supposed to do?"

"Does that radio work?" Truck didn't even have to look over his shoulder to see where the cop pointed his pen.

"Yeah."

"Maybe try that next time, huh? Now..." He looked down

at the citation pad in his mitt and prepared to write everything up.

"Excuse me, officer?" At the sound of her voice, both men looked up to find the girl leaning over the driver's seat on her palms. Her elbows were close, pressing her breasts together in a way that plumped them forward.

Ticket Dodging 101.

"Miss?"

"It's late, and we've been through a lot," she said. "I don't suppose you could let us off with a warning? I can promise you we'll radio if they come back." There was just enough flirtation in her voice to throw the whole thing sideways.

Officer By-The-Book sighed and sucked his teeth as he sized up the view she offered.

"Alright," he said at last, clicking the pen again. He looked at Truck, raising an eyebrow. "Kid sister, I suppose?"

"Guessed it in one," Truck smiled. "She wanted to see what life was like on the open road."

"Yeah, well." The cop snuffed out a snarky laugh. "Try to keep it less exciting from now on, huh?"

"Yes, sir." With that, Truck heaved himself back up into his seat, using every ounce of his willpower not to slam the door. "Now you can go back to sleep, fucker," he muttered before cutting his eyes back over to the girl. "You're something else, you know that?"

She just shrugged, smiling in a way that could read as either innocent or naughty, depending on which side of the gutter your mind was on.

"So, Mr. Laine…"

"Truck."

"Excuse me?" She looked legitimately thrown, and he softened up a bit, extending his hand.

"It's Tucker to my mom, but to everybody else, it's Truck."

"Violet." She took his hand, and that pesky little gyroscope went off in his gut.

Easy, Tiger. Don't get all keyed up.

"Alright, Violet," he said, cranking Layla to life again. "What are the chances those sons of bitches are watching us from somewhere out there in the tall grass?"

"Pretty good, I'd say." Her voice was faint, with just enough genuine sorrow in it to put him off his step.

"Well, only one way to find out." Shoving it into gear, Truck threw a lazy wave to the cop and pulled out onto the blacktop. Part of him toyed with chugging back towards the truck stop, but going backwards always rankled him. They'd already had one walk through the valley of the shadow of death, so what was another spin?

"Not much out here, is there?" It was a leading question, and he hoped it would knock the top off how this whole story got rolling.

"Precious little," she replied barely above a whisper.

Glancing over, he saw her resting her head on the window and gnawing at the cuticle of her thumb like it was a rare steak. There was enough trouble chasing this girl to set the world spinning backwards, but something about her brought out his protective side.

"Don't suppose you live around here?" he asked.

No answer.

Not that he was looking to get rid of her, but something had to give. He'd pulled his best Jack the Giant Killer act and plucked her out of the jaws of death – you'd think the girl would be willing to offer a bit of an explanation.

"Look, I don't want to pry into any of your business, but considering we just fought the battle of goddamn Waterloo without knowing each other's names, it seems like we should cover some basics, huh?" It came out a bit harder than he would have liked, but he was bone tired, and the bird of patience had flown south for the winter.

"I'm sorry, Mr.—"

"Truck."

"I'm sorry, Truck. And, I want you to know how grateful I am. Really." He looked at her, and those green eyes glistened with just enough water to dull his edges. "It's just I wish I hadn't dragged you into all this."

"You didn't drag me. I coulda just rolled on by and let you sort your own mess out, but that ain't me." This wasn't some chest puffing boast. Truck meant it to the soles of his feet.

"Thank you." The words were simple, but the feeling behind them sounded complicated as hell.

"Tricky question, but I'm gonna ask it anyway – how did all this start? Do you know any of those guys?"

"Tricky answer, but yes," she said. "They call themselves The Pack."

Of fucking course they do.

"What did they want?"

"Me."

Her answer hung between them like seven Salem witches.

There was no way under the sun or moon that Truck was gonna let them take her. Much as he hated to admit it, he'd staked his claim to her safety, and that's all there was to it.

"So, this Pack," he said. "I take it they had their paws on you before tonight?"

"Mm-hm." She nodded, keeping her thousand yard stare aimed at the windshield.

"For how long?"

"Listen, Truck, I really don't think you want to know any of this." She looked over to him, gimlet eyes brim full of weariness and too much sorrow for someone the shy side of twenty five. "I can't tell you how grateful I am you showed up, but this is a losing game."

"The only game I lose is checkers, and that's because I can't say no to my niece." Of all the miraculous things, the ragged redhead in his passenger seat laughed. Musical, and infectious enough that Truck joined in. "Alright," he said, "I'm not gonna pry too deep into things tonight."

"Thank you."

"Oh, don't misunderstand. If you're riding with me, there's gonna be talk. Driving in quiet is fine solo, but with another person in the cab, it can make a guy nuts."

"Makes sense."

"But for tonight, I'm just going to find a place for us to sack out." He rolled down his window and leaned his head into the cool air. When he saw the confusion on her face, he nodded lightly into the darkness. "Listening for engines." If Violet tried to hide her shudder, she did a lousy job of it.

Once he'd gone another fifteen miles or so, Truck turned off the highway again. After all the tumult, he took extra care to steer Layla gently over the shoulder and out into the plains. Just up ahead was another one of those butt-ugly billboards for The Whatever-The-Fuck, and Truck eased up along behind it. Half the lights pointed at the sign were busted, so he crossed his fingers it'd provide a wee bit of cover.

As they shuddered to a stop, Violet jolted up from what must have been a turbulent little dream. Truck hadn't even noticed her drifting off to sleep.

"It's okay," he said in his best reassuring voice. "Just hunkering down."

Leaning his seat back, he fetched up the lukewarm beer sweating through the koozie and cracked it open. Even shy of ice cold, it tasted like paradise. When his eyes found Violet's, they were fixed on the can with longing like something out of a storybook. A yearning "knights and damsels" kinda look.

"There's another one over there," he said, gesturing to the second beer across the cab. "Help yourself."

She looked at it and a bright smile crept over her face.

Simple pleasures mean deep things to complicated people.

Snapping the tab, she turned and raised the can to him. He toasted her back, and they drank in silence for a couple of minutes. The adrenaline was well and truly gone, and all that was left was the soul deep exhaustion of his long haul, doubled up with the Hazard County shit he'd just pulled.

Shifting to haul himself into the sleeping nook behind the seats, the waif in the passenger seat caught him up. That little protective demon clinging to the inside of his ribs whipped its tail up to sting the underside of his heart.

"Okay. Check it out." He nodded back to his little cave. "There's a bed back there that's more than a little comfortable. Sorry the sheets are on the rumpled side, but I always do laundry when I get home. Get back there and bunk out."

"No..." She pulled her knees up and pushed her back against the door. It looked weirdly defensive, and Truck sat perplexed for a moment. When it hit him, he snuffed out a smirking laugh.

"Shit, Violet, I'm not coming back there with you." He chuckled, and her shoulders dropped a mile. He raised three fingers and shot her a crooked smile. "Scout's honor. Won't be the first time I've slept in the front here. Besides, given I first saw you running from the fucking desert, I imagine it's been a hot minute since you've slept on an actual mattress. Now get back there. I'm not asking you, I'm telling you."

"Are you sure?" She let her legs down, and leaned forward to peer into his dominion.

"Yup." He nodded. "Clothes on the passenger side are clean, so if you want you can help yourself to a tee shirt or something."

Up to now he'd only snagged small looks at her, but now that the dust had settled, he saw how tiny she really was. Half starved, probably. Just some little bird fluttering like hell to beat the wind. It only stoked his need to keep her safe from... whatever The Pack wanted.

"Thank you." She squeezed his knee, and looked for a second like she might say something else. In the end, she settled for another little, "Thank you," and scuttled into the back.

Truck leaned against his door and put his feet up in the passenger seat, sipping his warming beer. A rustle of fabric told him Violet was stripping down to take him up on the tee shirt offer.

Now, Truck was never a peeper, so the little wriggle of temptation to look unsettled him.

Under other circumstances, he might just have climbed into the back and humped the life out of her – if she was into it, that is – but this wasn't other circumstances. This wasn't flirty Heather from the truck stop. His rig had been host to several midnight rambles, but this wasn't that kind of party. He'd be goddamned if he spoiled it by getting all grabby. Even if she dragged him back there herself.

Polishing off the beer to drown the treacherous fucker trying to tug his gaze to the back, he leaned his head against the window and closed his eyes. It felt dangerously close to keeping watch. Which, in a way, it was.

He hadn't known Violet an hour, but he was already certain he'd beat the tarpaper out of anyone who so much as scuffed her shoe.

As such, the front seat was likely the best place to sleep anyway. If he was gonna play guard, might as well go full tilt. At that thought, he reached into the console and pulled out the pistol he kept to solve life's bigger problems, then leaned back to look up at the waxing moon. If anything came for the girl, he'd be ready for it.

There was no telling just what brand of bananas he'd fallen into, but he was in it to the last peel.

The gentle, cradle rocking of the rig eased Violet back to the land of the living. Truck was right about it being a hot minute since she'd spent a night in a bed, and she slept like she'd fallen into a coma. Rolling onto her back to stretch amidst the tangle of sheets, she half regretted finding herself alone. Which shocked her.

Violet had spent the better part of her life since puberty doing everything she could to sidestep the myriad assortment of guys crawling all over themselves to fuck her.

Ah, to be a woman in this world.

After over a decade of that kind of shit, it seemed like she might have tripped backwards into the bed of the only true gentleman on the planet – and all she wanted was to wake up with him next to her.

Get it together, girl. You can't keep thinking like this.

Which was true. Never in her life had she felt all the little twittery feelings she read about, but the magnetism of this truck driver had her at sixes and sevens. At the heart of it, the fact that he *hadn't* presumed upon her late-night hours was the very thing that made him so goddamn attractive.

Well, among the things.

Shuffling across his mattress, she fetched her jeans and

wriggled into them. For a second, she considered stripping off his tee to crawl back into her own sweat stained shirt, but thought better of it. His was clean, comfortable, and if she was being honest, she liked having an aspect of him so close to her. So, she knotted it at her waist and pulled her rumpled flannel back over her shoulders.

A sudden stab of sorrow caught her in the ribs. These threadbare clothes were all she had in the world. Not that she'd ever really had all that much to begin with – running with The Pack wasn't about accumulating *things* – and yet, she would have sorely liked at least a change of socks. Fresh underwear would have been a luxury worthy of Midas.

Taking a deep breath to try and dispel a scrap of angst, she got up into the passenger seat.

"Good morning."

"Good morning," he said, an enigmatic smile tucked just under the corners of his mustache. Seeing his face in the daylight, Violet was certain it had visited her dreams. If only she could remember how. "I hope you slept well?"

"So well," she said. "How about you?" He shrugged in answer and drummed his thumb on the wheel.

Bright sunlight glared off the interstate stretching out to the horizon. She leaned back, and a queasy sparkle settled behind her breastbone. She liked the easy quiet, but maybe she was reading it wrong.

Was it possible she was presuming too much about him?

"What's the plan?" she asked cautiously.

He gave her a sideways glance by way of reply, and pointed toward a green mileage sign on the point of whizzing past.

"Next town that's worth a damn is in about eight miles. It's small, but it should be safe enough for you."

Violet's chest went cold, and her heart withered to dust.

Just for me?

Before she could catch herself, a treacherous little voice inside her cried out in misery.

I'm going to lose him.

Not that he was ever hers to keep.

In the movies, cowboys always ride away, so she should just be grateful for the rescue and the good night's sleep. Besides, pulling him headlong into her world of bullshit was seven different kinds of cruel. True or not, it hadn't stopped her from wanting it.

Hugging one leg up onto the seat, she rested her chin on her knee and looked out. Despite spending the better part of her life in the wild, scrubby open, it all looked the same to her.

Surely she ought to be able to pick out every landmark like some kind of frontier trapper, right?

Nope.

To her it was all just dirt.

Low rising hills studded with mesquite scrub paced lazily by outside. Acres of sky so blue it stung if you looked at it too long. Nothing but cactus, caliche, and bad memories stretched out to the horizon.

The eight miles went by in a blur of white lines, and the horizon broke over the skyline of a town that wished it was big enough to be small. Regardless, as they rolled into it, it boasted the kind of self-consciously folksy charm that all these little fly bitten towns ginned up to sell postcards.

The main street was just this side of a ghost town, and they managed to find a stretch on the main square that didn't look like they'd get arrested if they stowed the rig there for a spell. And, as it was directly across from the police station, if parking was a jailable offense, they'd find out in pretty short order.

At the sight of the station, Violet's body melted into a puddle of ice water. Truck couldn't just drop her off there, right? Was that the "someplace safe" he'd mentioned?

It couldn't be. He didn't seem like the kind of guy to just dump her into the swollen, porky fingers of some backwater smokies and ride off into the sunset.

A billion things bubbled up in her ragged, dust scorched throat. There was too much to explain, and no way to spill it all out without sounding like a complete nutcase. If she were to tell the truth, the whole truth, and nothing but the truth, she wouldn't just wind up in a cell – they'd toss her in a padded room and flush the key down the toilet.

"Jesus, are you okay?"

She didn't even realize she was shivering until his voice washed over her. Even her teeth were chattering, so she clamped her jaw shut and swallowed around the steel walnut in her throat.

"I think so." Violet looked into his face with her best imploring eyes and tried to read anything in him other than goodbye. "Should I get out?"

"You're gonna have to," he said.

Oh, no.

Her mouth went dry and sticky, and stinging tears crept into her eyes.

"I don't know your sizes." He chuckled, digging into his pocket to peel off a couple of bills. Blinking hard, Violet gulped the lump in her throat down.

"My sizes?"

"Yeah." He shot her a knit-browed, quizzical look and pointed out her window. There, just next to the police station, was a little store selling pretty much everything but groceries and hardware. "Figure you could use something that hasn't been lived in for weeks. Let's face it – your jeans are toast, and it looks like you've already claimed one of my shirts."

She let out a sigh, and her whole body unraveled in an instant. Violet shook her head, and an exhausted laugh burbled up out of her gut.

Is this guy for real? Where the hell did he come from?

"You didn't think I was dropping you off with the blue boys, did you?" He nodded to the side, and she followed the line to see one of the city's finest lounging on a bench outside the station. "I mean," Truck snorted, "does that guy look like a life saver to you?"

The cop was the size of an oil drum with none of the charm. Beached on his bench, he eyed the two unwelcome guests like he was looking for any reason in the world to write them up.

"Just take this," Truck said, holding out a small wad of cash. "I'll sit with the rig in case T.J. Hooker over there gets any ideas." Exploding into a smile, Violet took the proffered bills. To her tender eyes, forty bucks might as well have been a monopoly bag. It was the first time she'd held actual money in ages.

"Thank you," she said, and Truck just nodded and leaned back in his seat. Feeling like things might finally be breaking her way, Violet opened the door and started to slide out into the muggy heat that swelled in to meet her.

She didn't even hear the shots.

Instinct made her jerk her legs up, and a trio of bullet holes punched daylight through the passenger door. Everything went into slow motion. She looked back to see the very thing that she'd been dreading. Pure, primal terror flooded her whole system.

Oh, fuck.

It was Scum.

The Pack's scout.

Of course he had been tailing them. Probably self-appointed.

To say he was the wild card in The Pack didn't even touch the unspeakable mayhem that followed him around. His feral, unpredictable nature rendered him the most dangerous figure in a whole host of treacherous monsters.

Case in point: The sun was shining right down the middle of the morning, and Scum was in Full Wolf.

It's not like there were edicts against it, but the general rule of thumb was that you didn't Wolf out unless you knew nobody was going to live to spread that shit around. Judging by the look in his horrible yellow eyes, he didn't give a good goddamn one way or the other. As if to punctuate the fact, he leaned back and pealed out a terrible howl.

This time she heard the crack of the gun, and was able to move her legs before another bullet hole sprang up near the door handle.

Scum strode up Main Street, boot heels clicking, chains rattling, pistol in his claws, and slaver dripping from his ravenous mouth.

All at once, Violet jerked backwards, yanked by the powerful hand of Truck Laine. The rig blazed to life and jolted into motion before the engine had fully turned over. They pitched forward, and just before momentum slammed her door, Violet caught a glimpse of the hefty officer writhing on his bench. The fat fucker kicked his heels, trying to shove himself to standing and unfasten his gun at the same time as donut crumbs scattered down his chest.

"Get down," Truck grunted, pushing her shoulder until Violet crouched between the seats next to the console. "You know how to load a clip?" She looked up into his steely face and nodded. "Good." He pounded his fist in a strategic spot on the dash, and the glove box fell open. "You'll find a box of ammo and two extra clips in there. Get to it."

Blinking for an instant, she somehow missed the moment when a pistol materialized in his hand.

"It's no good," she said. Truck's eyes flashed to her.

"What?"

"They're useless unless they're silver." The words were out in the open before she could clap a hand over her mouth to stop them, and a look of unalloyed bewilderment surged over Truck's face. Turning to squint hard into his side mirror, his jaw hit his chest and he whipped his astonished gaze back to her.

"You've got to be fucking kidding me."

"If only," she said, cowering in place.

"Son of a bitch."

He slammed on the gas, and the rig launched like a rocket down the centerline of Tumbleweed Avenue.

The good thing about most small towns is that the roads are so straight you can tear ass from one end to the other without so much as touching your wheel. The shitty thing is that the roads are straight, so it's a real fucker to try and find a place to hide from a gunman.

A volley of shots broke the morning behind them, and Violet pressed her nose to the window to watch in the rear view mirror. The porcine Barney Fife stood legs akimbo, pumping round after round at Scum, just like he was taught in the Academy. The beast kept walking, taking the hits with a terrifying pride. Knowing what was coming, Violet looked away before a swipe of Scum's claws slashed the poor fucker to hell.

"How are those clips coming?" Truck's voice snapped her back to face him.

"I told you they're no good."

"Humor me," he said, shifting gears and slamming the gas harder. Biting down, she started stuffing ammo into the clip.

If it doesn't kill them, maybe it will at least slow them down.

"Jesus shit," Truck mumbled. She didn't even have to look.

The telltale savage pop of engines told her that Scum hadn't gone rogue after all.

There were others.

They must've come out ahead in ambush. From the dusty side streets streamed beastly, desert rusted choppers, each one serving as noble steed to leather clad Wolves. They would have looked nightmarish in the darkness, but the morning sun painted them with the surreal brush of undeniable fact.

Sirens went up, and the melee got into full swing. Violet hated that the police were marching straight into the gaping, insatiable mouth of death, but a dark part of her was grateful. With a parade of cops adding to the confusion, The Pack's attention might be divided enough for Truck and Violet to get the drop on the situation. Or at least a little perspective.

"I need to ask you something, Violet," Truck said, his voice gruff. "Look at me." She did, and those hypnotic, dark eyes had gone hard. "Was that a fucking Werewolf?"

Her throat tightened and words skittered off until all she could do was nod.

"Un-fucking-real," he grunted.

She wanted to shrivel up and die. Truck was a good guy, and she'd wrenched him into a whole level of misery most people didn't deserve to see – especially folks who gave a hoot in hell about strangers in peril. But, now that he'd seen the truth, he was in this. Like it or not. And she knew the answer was definitely *not*.

FIVE

This was the kind of shit they didn't teach in truck driving school.

Steering onto a runaway ramp when the brakes failed on mountain roads?

Yup.

How to keep from hydroplaning into an overpass during a monsoon?

You got it.

Leading a gang of motorcycle riding Werewolves on a mad chase into the heart of the desert?

Somehow, they missed that one in the manual.

Truck had to ask himself: *If I'd known this last night, would I have scooped this girl up?* He cut a look at the tough-as-nails sparrow folded up in the passenger seat stuffing bullets into clips, and the answer came without so much as a hiccup.

Fuckin' A right I would.

"I've got them loaded," Violet said, clutching the magazines in front of her. "Give me the gun, and I'll reload."

"Hang on," Truck said, rolling down his window. "Let me empty it out first."

Clamping an iron hand on the center of the steering

wheel, he craned into the whipping wind and spied eight motorcycles charging up his left flank.

Now, Truck had never been much of a crack shot with his left hand. Not that he was shooting buffalo nickels at sixty paces with his right, but he could hold his own when the time was right. But the current time was definitely wrong, so his southpaw hip shots were just going to have to do.

Blasting off a few rounds didn't do a damn thing, so clearly it was time to strategize. With no other options worth a damn, he settled for shooting at the one thing he knew he could hit.

The road.

Pulling the trigger like he was dispensing Pez, Truck dumped a brace of bullets square at the blacktop, sending ricochets whizzing up towards the rotten monsters bearing down on him. A pretty wild tactic, but he must have scored a hit or two because they eased right the hell back.

"There's only so long this can last," he said, sliding back into his seat and fixing his attention on the highway ahead. They were coming up on a curve, and he needed to hug into the oncoming lane to keep their pursuers from shooting up past them on the inside track.

Trouble was, there was a line of lazy traffic piddling along in the lane he needed to steal.

"Hang on."

She already was. One hand on the oh-shit bar, and the other seconds away from ripping the stuffing out of the side of her seat. Braced for impact.

Smart girl.

Hitting his hazard lights, Truck reached up to rattle down the walls of Jericho with his horn. If those poor sons of bitches didn't get out of his way, they were liable to have a lousy afternoon.

"Sorry, folks," he muttered as he seized the left lane and hugged the shoulder like a newlywed bride.

Sedans and sport utility wagons leapt into the scrum, kicking up clouds of choking dust. Others broke wide and zoomed along his passenger side, honking like it was supposed to make a goddamn difference.

Jesus help them when they ran into the party trailing behind Layla's tail lights.

Deaf to all the bullshit, Truck white knuckled it around the curve so fast, Layla threatened to go ass over teakettle. If that happened, they'd be in a whole different world of trouble.

Layla buckled and whined, and for a split second, Truck could have sworn a couple of her trailer tires left the ground, but he managed to keep the old girl from turning into a roadside attraction.

"Now you're talking," he shouted as they finally broke back into the clear. Adrenaline sang in his veins like Pavoratti. He'd put Layla in some sticky spots in her time, but coming out the other side of this without so much as a fender scratch sent his stomach into a Super Bowl end zone dance.

The view ahead wasn't half bad either. The road in front of them was one long, straight line to the horizon. Perfect for gaining ground, even if it was dogshit when it came to duck-and-cover prospects.

"Oh, no," Violet whimpered from the passenger seat.

"What?"

"Um..." She turned to him, abject terror shining in her eyes.

Looking in his rear view, Truck caught sight of a tow truck charging up behind him. At the wheel sat a glowering Wolf, tongue hanging out over jagged fangs.

"Are they gonna ram me?"

The answer came back quick, and negative.

It pulled up so close on Truck's back end, a dime couldn't drop between the bumpers. Then it laid the bed down until it scraped the pavement, sending up enough sparks to start a brushfire that would burn for fifty years.

"What the fuck?"

It's a fucking ramp!

The screaming buzzsaw of an engine called out above the rest, and a bike peeled plumb up the middle, zoomed along the bed of the tow truck, and sailed through the air. The lupine Evel Knievel practically winked at Truck as it torpedoed across the cloudless sky. A split second later, an ugly screech and thump told Truck exactly what brand of trouble they were in.

"He's up top."

They had a Werewolf on top of the rig, and that meant only one kind of news – bad.

"Shit," Truck spat. There wasn't even an overpass ahead where he could try to scrape the devil off. "I know I said this already, but hang on." Violet's knuckles were so taut the bones might punch through any second.

Stealing another look in his rear views, Truck caught sight of a smattering of motorcycles on either side. *Cool,* he thought. *I get a bonus out of this.* Jerking the wheel left, then right, he almost fishtailed the trailer in an effort to shake their unwelcome visitor off the top.

No dice.

Truck did, however, manage to clean the clocks of one or two Werewolf lampreys, so it wasn't a total loss. If he slammed on the brakes, it might send the tick on their back flying, but the side effect would put them square in the middle of the hoard. Which was a death trap if ever there was one.

"Shit," Truck muttered. He knew what he was going to have to do, he just didn't want to admit it to himself. Too bad for him, there was no time for denial. He was gonna have to eat this plate of shit while it was hot.

"Violet, I'm gonna need you to do me a favor."

"Anything." Her quick reply made him cut his eyes over sharply.

"Don't agree so fast to something you're not gonna like," he said, then gave a tight nod. "I need you to take the wheel."

"What?" She shrank to half her size. "Why?"

"I'm going up."

Her jaw fell open in disbelief.

"Truck, you can't!"

"It ain't a question of what I can or can't do. No choice here, unless you want that shithead down here with us in about thirty seconds. Now, just head straight up the center line, and if you spot anybody coming from the other direction, blow the horn. Got it?"

"Got it." All the color drained out of her face, and she sat shaking like a date on prom night. Anybody else might have made Truck reconsider, but something about this girl told him she was up to it – whether she looked the part or not.

They snapped off their belts at the same time, and he pulled her onto his lap.

"Feel the gas?" he asked. She nodded. "Keep it right there. If anything happens, the clutch is on the left. You ever drive a stick?"

She pulled her lips tight and shook her head no.

Goddamnit.

"You'll be a natural," he assured her. "Trust me."

She felt like a million dollars cash on his lap, and there were about as many reasons as there were pennies in that number for him to want to keep her there. But, he needed his head in the game, and focusing on a tight bottom nestled up against his midsection wasn't going to be much use in that department. So, he eased out from under her and heaved his torso through the window.

"Fuck!" One of those Wolf bastards was right there, pacing them. Reaching back into the cab, Truck made a grabby hand for the gun. The whole time he hung eye to eye with the slobbering monster, the whipping wind doing its dead level best to fling him right into its waiting jaws.

The beast gunned its motor, eyes gleaming above what had to pass for a sneering smile. It wore a sleeveless leather vest, caked with sweat, blood, piss and god knows what else, its shaggy arms roped with lean, fight-club muscle. Working its fingers on the handlebars, Truck could see long, nasty claws jutting out the end of every single one. A single swipe and this whole story would be over.

Truck sped up his grippy hand.

"The gun," he hissed without taking his eyes off the monster across from him. It snarled in his face, sending up a waft of fetid breath. "The gun," Truck barked louder.

There it was. Cold metal, and that satisfying sandpapery grip.

In one fluid motion, he snatched his arm out, leveled it at the reeking, vicious muzzle, and pulled the trigger. The head snapped back with a yelp, and the bike jerked and flipped into the scrub.

Silver or not, it was nice to know that good old lead still had some sting to it. The Wolf might not be dead, but he was in for more than a garden variety hangover.

A howl from above snatched Truck's attention back to why this whole mess of hanging out the window got started.

There, standing on the corner of his trailer, was the same rangy Wolf who had shot up his door back in Sleepyville. Tattered shreds of clothing billowed in the wind, and its fur slapped and blustered all over hell and back.

Pointing his gun up, Truck took a wild shot and missed by a country mile. The thing ducked back and disappeared over the edge of the rig, keeping Truck on the unlucky path of dragging himself up onto Layla's silvery spine. Staying as at the ready as he could, Truck clambered out and pulled himself on top of the cab. Getting from there to the trailer was going to be a whole other thing, but at least if he stood to his full height, he could peer over and get the lay of the land.

The Wolf was on all fours, a coiled up copperhead ready to strike. Truck fired again, and it only hunkered lower. Casting a quick eye over his shoulder, Truck ensured that there was still plenty of straight road ahead.

It was now or never.

He fired a series of rapid shots, hoping to put his enemy off center enough for him to climb up.

It worked, but only to a point.

The thing retreated to the far end of the rig, taking cover behind the bike lying on its side. Truck jumped, and managed to get his upper half on the roof. Getting his legs high enough to gain purchase was another story.

The Wolf stood. Shoulders back, tilting its head as it studied its prey, then leaned back to let out a deafening howl. The sound echoed across the plains as the Wolf closed on Truck with deliberate steps.

Truck was in a world of shit because every time he tried to line up a shot to buy himself some time, he lost ground hauling himself up.

Some grand fucking idea this turned out to be.

At last he got a knee up, but the Wolf was right on top of him. Kicking his leg as hard as he could, Truck rolled onto his back, pointing his gun straight up and pulling the trigger. Another miss, but it sent the fiend on the retreat again.

Breathing hard from his climb, Truck stood up and got his balance against the wind. From up there he could see all the way to the last squad car. There was plenty of trouble on the ground, but there was an on-the-level problem that needed handling first.

The brute hunched behind the bike, glaring at Truck with eyes boiling in blood. *Say goodnight, asshole,* Truck thought, lining up his shot.

Click.

"Oh, for fuck's sake."

He pulled the trigger again. Nothing. He should have gotten another clip before starting this ruckus. Evidently, an empty gun is a siren song to Werewolves because that bastard came out ready to party.

Springing forward, it swiped a razor sharp paw at Truck's chest, and our hero only just managed to duck it. The thing staggered past with the momentum, giving Truck a prime shot at the ribs, which he gladly took. The solid punch elicited a canine yawp, and Truck steeled himself for whatever counterattack was in the offing.

A quick slash sent Truck staggering backwards, grateful it only managed to rip his shirt. He'd seen the movies, and he wasn't in any hurry to get all hairy himself because of a teeny little scratch.

It lunged again and again, backing Truck all the way down the length of his rig. In short order, his heels were at the rear edge. Squaring up, he could almost swear he saw the vile brute smile. It lowered its shoulders, scraping his boot on the top of the trailer like a bull ready to charge. Which is exactly what it did.

A terrible roar rattled up from the deepest part of its chest as it made for Truck. At the last second, Truck dropped flat on his stomach and grabbed the Wolf's ankles. It tripped up, fumbled a step or two, then let out a terrible scream as it cratered out of sight over the back of the rig.

Truck heard it hit the pavement like a garbage bag full of raw beef. Coming to his feet, he saw the chaos of bikes dodging and peeling past their fallen brother.

He had to do something to get things back in some kind of shape. Just next to him was the unruly scrub brush motorcycle the beast jumped up with, lying on its side like a sleeping dragon.

In an instant it was up, and Truck cranked on it until it roared to ungodly life. Standing beside it, he wrenched at the throttle until it bucked under his hands. Ripping a sleeve from his shirt, he knocked off the gas cap, stuffed the cloth in, and sparked it with his Zippo. It blazed up pretty quickly, turning the damn thing into a bomb on wheels.

Another couple of revs for good measure, and Truck turned it loose to soar down onto the trailing army. It hit the ground and detonated into a fireball, sending up a lick of flame like the devil's bullwhip. A gout of pungent, black smoke swirled up after it, followed by more intense fire.

Just as Truck planned, the fracas behind him lost focus and crumbled in on itself.

Alright. We're ahead by one.

For now.

SIX

With all the dreadful noises echoing down from the top of the eighteen wheeler, Violet had a hell of a time keeping her eyes on the road.

Every howl, crash, and grunt curdled her stomach into uglier and uglier knots. It was one thing for The Pack to send their scout out in Full Wolf under the morning sun, but ramping Scum onto a moving big rig?

It was one of two things – desperation, or white-hot rage. Knowing how The Duke ruled his mangy army, Violet had a razor keen idea which one it was.

What if Scum wins?

The thought was too hideous to bear. Bad news was, no matter how deep she buried it, it came wriggling back to the surface.

To her, Truck looked like he'd been kicking asses since diaper days, but this level of pandemonium would be outside of just about anybody's wheelhouse. The notion of Scum's repulsive face lunging in through the window was enough to cover her in a sheen of cold sweat.

An explosion made her jump so hard, she all but busted her head on the ceiling. Biting down, she clung to the wheel like a Titanic life preserver, and burned a hole in the road ahead with her stare.

Don't look back, she told herself, terrified of what she'd find.

Besides, the straightaway Truck had pointed the rig up was rapidly giving way to a canyon, and Violet didn't relish the idea of reeling down those treacherous roads on her own.

Every second behind the wheel put her a hundred feet closer to having to do just that.

"Make way."

Oh, thank God.

It was Truck.

He planted his boots on the window ledge, and she swung her hips out of the captain's chair to make room. Her foot came off the gas, and the world slowed on its axis. With one fluid movement, Truck secured himself in the driver's seat, and Violet thumped back into the passenger side to watch him.

His sleeve was torn, and she feasted her eyes on the cables of muscle running up his arm. He was shiny with sweat, and his chest heaved mightily – but he was whole.

Gloriously, irresistibly whole.

"Are you...?"

Before he could get another word out, she was on him. It may have been a rash impulse, but she flung herself across the cab, took his face in her eager hands, and kissed him with everything she had. Her lips burned under his instant of hesitation, then his mouth answered. Firm, ardent pressure, and then a light, sucking graze of her lower lip between his teeth.

The impulsive kiss was lightning strike fast, but the thunder of desire rumbled between them long after she pulled back. His eyes were equal parts shock and hunger. Then, with a hard blink, he turned back to the road.

Just in time, as it happens. The first bend of the canyon

was dead ahead, and Violet scrunched back into her seat and buckled in. The rig shook under his feathered braking, and she marveled at the intense pressure of the trailer pushing forward as Truck worked to slow the thing down. If he didn't, that kind of momentum would pitch them clean over the dropoff.

They made the bend, and Violet looked past Truck's granite profile to see the seething wreckage out his window. A noxious billow of smoke snaked up into the sky, surrounded by a tangle of figures under the glare of flashing lights.

In an instant, they ducked around a crag and the whole bloody business vanished behind them. But it was far from out of sight, out of mind. Violet knew better than that. They may have slipped the madness in the rear-view mirror, but just like the little decal said, that shit was always closer than it appeared.

Evening was gaining on them fast when Truck pulled off the road and eased the rig through some brush. Violet's whole body stood at attention, the gentle rocking of the cab doing jack squat to sing a lullaby to the acid in her gut.

"What are we doing?" she asked.

"Hiding," Truck replied. It was the first word he'd said in what felt like eternity, and clouds hung over it. After her impulsive kiss, things had gone quiet. So quiet there'd been moments Violet would have sold an army of firstborn children to get a peek into his brain.

Snugged into a ravine with less than three feet of clearance on either side, Truck killed the engine, flicked off his seatbelt, and turned to face her square on. His eyes were unreadable in a way that terrified and excited her all at once.

"Alright," he said. "Time to fucking spill."

Her blood frosted over.

There were so many things to say.

Too many.

He'd seen the tip of the iceberg, but how would she ever be able to lead him all the way to the bottom? Clearly, her hesitation wasn't welcome, and he raked a hand through his hair.

"Look." He huffed out a weary sigh. "I'm not mad. Yet. But I think you'd agree I deserve some answers. Now, I don't regret pulling you out of that mess last night, but I didn't know how deep the shit was until I was already up to my waist. Girl on the run from bikers? That's ugly. But fucking Werewolves? We're on the other side of the looking glass on this one, you feel me?"

"Yes." Her voice tasted small in her mouth. Breathing in hard, she gripped her knees and looked for a way in. "It's the first time I've ever tried to get away from The Pack."

"You've been in the clutches of those assholes for a while?"

Longer than I can say.

She nodded.

"For a long time." The thread of her breath ran thin as a hair, but she could tell from Truck's disposition that he'd wait until she could knit it into something. "I've been out in the desert for most of my life. And The Pack is a kind of roving kingdom. The Duke..." she shuddered even saying his title out loud. "He's the one at the top."

"That the guy who pulled a stunt jump onto old Layla here?" he asked, thumping the dash with his fist. Violet shook her head.

"That was Scum. This is going to sound insane, but he's the crazy one. The scout. The lowest of the low, but The Pack can't do without him because he does all the worst stuff. The dangerous stuff."

"I figured that part out." Truck shifted in his seat, some of the steel slipping out of his spine. "Where's this Duke?"

"I haven't seen him," she admitted. "He never gets his hands dirty unless he means business."

"Cute." Truck swiped a palm over his forehead and up over his crown of hair, stealing a look through the windshield. "Good to know we're not official business."

For her part, Violet was actually surprised not to have seen The Duke yet. Especially given *she* was the one all the fuss was about.

"Why now?" Truck asked, turning his attention back to her. "Why run?"

"One of them tried to claim me." The word, *claim* nearly choked her. Because this wasn't some wedding-bell-blues brand of hitching up. This was being fucked against her will on a cactus for the rest of her miserable life. Once one of them had her, she was bound to him from then on.

"I take it that wasn't your buddy Scum either?" Truck asked.

"No," Violet said, a fresh spasm of disgust rippling through her. "It was The Chamberlain. The Duke's second."

"These guys have a whole list of colorful names, huh?" The sardonic humor in his voice snagged like barbed wire under her skin, and he must have seen the hurt on her face because his whole demeanor softened. "What happened?"

"They were back from a hunt. It's always a party after that, and somehow The Chamberlain managed to get me alone. I've learned to be pretty good about making sure I'm never on my own with any of them, but that son of a bitch is sneaky. He singled me out. I'd barely even realized it before he laid me over his lap on his bike and drove us out... somewhere. I was kicking and trying to scream, but he just kept pushing my head down. Telling me to shut up. We finally stopped, and when he undid his pants, I yanked them down to his ankles, threw dirt in his face, kicked him in the dick, and ran."

She didn't realize her face was wet until Truck stuffed a Kleenex into her palm.

"You're a resourceful one, you know that?"

"Well," she shrugged. "I'd been around them long enough to know where the dirty tricks hide."

"Seems so." Truck nodded. "Look, I don't know how this whole thing pans out, but I'm gonna do everything in my power not to let them get to you." Her gaze flashed up to his, and something enigmatic sparkled behind the dark of his eyes.

Suddenly, all she wanted was to kiss him again. The first one had come on sheer animal impulse, but now a mix of new things jostled around in her guts. It felt a lot like need, and the power of it scared her so much her heart bolted like a rabbit.

"You can't make a promise like that," she said, trying to disappear into herself. "It's bad enough you're in this far, I can't let you get in any deeper. Best to just let me out and go."

"Hey." Suddenly he was on his knees between the seats, his fingers clamped on her thighs. Those eyes mere inches from her, close enough to see that they weren't black, but hazelnut brown. His voice came soft and warm, "No way I'm letting you go. The second I pulled you up into Layla here, I was in this. I'll be goddamned if I just put you out and run. Werewolves or no."

Violet's heart strained against her ribs. She put her hands on top of his, and ran them slowly up his arms. A furtive flicker shot over his face as she looked back and forth between his eyes and his lips.

He was looking at her lips too.

Neither of them moved, but the space between them grew smaller and smaller by faint degrees. Violet's breath was high and hoarse, just below her collarbone. When their mouths finally found each other, all that air collected into a vibrating moan coursing up her throat and into his.

Sliding forward, she perched on the edge of the seat and pressed her knees toward each other, relishing the feel of his firm body between her thighs. Truck's powerful hands slid up along her legs, fretting across the curve of her ass with the barest caress, then up her back to cradle her.

They pulled into each other, deepening the kiss. Liquid heat pooled up at the base of Violet's stomach, and she clung to him hard. She grabbed a fistful of his hair and kissed him as if the world was on fire. As if she were drowning, and he was both the sea and the air at the same time.

"Listen," Truck said, breaking the kiss. "We... um..." His voice was thick as molasses, pouring over her with delicious leisure. "We need to keep our heads straight."

"We do."

"There's still trouble out there." He stole another series of small kisses.

"There is," she whispered into his lips.

"What we need is rest. No need to rush into things."

When he peeled back from her, Violet's whole body radiated longing at his absence. Opening her heavy lidded eyes, she found him sitting back on his heels, looking at her like a steak dinner.

"Rest," she mumbled. "Yes."

With superhuman effort, she turned away from him and crept into the back of the cab. Slipping out of her jeans, she unfastened her bra and pulled it off under her shirt.

His shirt.

As she curled back into the safety of her den, she looked to find Truck still kneeling next to the console, looking off in perfect profile.

"Are you coming?" she asked quietly. His head snapped to look at her. "Just to rest."

She meant it, but offered a coy smile to season the invitation. Truck turned back to his seat, and she heard the locks go. Then, he stuffed a fresh clip into his gun and eased back to join her.

The heat of him in that small space overwhelmed her. The intoxicating smell of him sent her head swimming, and she lay in electric expectation, fully open to whatever this man might offer.

"Roll onto your side," he whispered. She did, and he molded himself around her, enveloping her in his arms. All the knots in her back melted against his rock hard chest, and she surrendered to the shape of him. Her head resting on his bicep, she snuggled closer and felt the hardness in his jeans.

Easy. Just breathe.

A row of delicate kisses traced up the line of her neck, finally coming to a stop just behind her ear.

"Get some sleep," he purred. "You're safe. I've got you."

And she was out.

SEVEN

Truck woke with a start.

One of the many top-shelf accolades Truck could offer his little den behind the seats was it did a damn fine job of keeping out the morning sun. Back in that dim cave, he could outsleep Rip Van Winkle if he had the inclination.

It had been an asset on countless mornings, but in light of the wholesale insanity he'd tripped backwards into, it wasn't exactly ideal. Not with the chance that he'd wake to a crowd of fucking Wolfmen glaring through the windshield.

And yet, as his nostrils filled with a scent that made every inch of him quake – some inches more than others – he might have called an even trade.

He inhaled deeply, letting the smell of the sleeping girl smooth over all the cracks their situation roiled open. Curling forward, he wrapped himself around the delicate young woman burrowed against him.

When he was ready to peel his eyes open, he let his gaze linger over her. Still wandering somewhere in dreamland, Violet looked old beyond her years. She couldn't have been more than twenty five, but every goddamn year was hard won. Even so, she was beautiful in a way that made his stomach hurt.

Even with all the nightmare creatures that should have haunted his dreams, being next to her was enough for Truck to sleep the sleep of the innocent. Heavenly as it was, lounging in the half-light with her wasn't an option. Not with hell waiting for them on the plains.

If they wanted to live, it was time for him to get moving.

The memory of a thousand jagged teeth infesting gaping red mouths crowded into the tiny space. Glaring sets of demonic eyes shimmered in his imagination with absurd, impossible reality.

Fucking Werewolves, he thought. *Now I've seen everything.*

Hidden as they were, he still had to face the fact that those bastards were out there somewhere, and he was going to have to meet the day one way or the other.

Violet murmured slightly as he slipped his arm out from under her head, replacing it with a fistful of clean tee shirts. She snuggled down into them, and Truck made sure she was out again, then grabbed his gun and picked his way out to the front of his cab as quietly as possible. It was broad day, and he chambered a round, peering through the windows in search of company.

If any of those scruffy dirtbags were around, they were playing a varsity league game of hide-and-seek. Never one to trust to dumb luck, Truck winced as he cracked the driver's side door and hopped down onto the sun baked dirt.

Dropping into an immediate squat, he looked under the truck for any stray legs or wheels that might give away unwelcome guests.

So far as he could see, he and Violet were on their own.

Satisfied, Truck stood to his full height and made his way down along Layla's side towards the rear. No doubt about it, the lady had some battle scars – a testament to the gonzo reality of the previous day's festivities.

"Sorry, girl," Truck muttered as he ran the flat of his hand along a particularly nasty gouge in her once pristine side. "I'll make it up to you. I promise."

Things didn't look much better when he got around the back. The rear doors had all the charm of a shooting gallery on Fourth of July weekend. Giving it a solid gander, Truck admitted to himself that the whole trailer might just end up a wash. And he wasn't exactly wallowing in the dough to snag himself a new one.

There wasn't much aftermarket value for a trailer scarred up from a fucking Werewolf battle. That said, if he was able to find a buyer willing to swallow the tale, he might just be sitting on a goldmine.

"Whatever," he grunted as he undid the padlock that kept the latches in place. "I'll figure it out later." Lifting the handle and giving a solid pull, he screeched the right door open enough to hoist himself inside.

Looking back one more time, he squinted down the rest of the canyon. The last thing he wanted was to be at the far end of a steel box if somebody got a notion to surprise him.

There was no sign of trouble, so with an uncomfortable shrug he turned to head into the bowels of Layla's hold. As always after a run, it was one long echoey coffin, with a few tiedown straps scattered across the floor.

Striding all the way up to the front, Truck came upon the battered wooden tool chest he'd bolted to the floor the day he signed the paperwork. He kicked it open, and there waiting for him was a trusty sidekick from his rowdier days.

"Hey, there," he said, bending down to pick up a well-used shotgun. "Miss me?"

He hadn't been at the butt end of Pepper in too goddamn long, and all he could think was how much help she would have been less than twenty four hours earlier.

There's no use crying over spilt motor oil, so he tucked the gun up under his arm and grabbed as many boxes of shells as he could carry. He had a sneaking suspicion that gunfire was going to become a way of life for the next little bit, and this boomstick was factory built to clear a path.

A quick check told him that Pepper was fully loaded and ready for business, which went a fair stretch to making him feel better about the day ahead. That said, even if every pellet in the whole caboodle was sterling, it wouldn't do a damn bit of good on two empty stomachs. He dumped the whole mess in the driver's seat and set about slapping something together.

In the cab, he was able to rustle up a can of Spam, some powdered eggs, water, and his trusty hotplate. On those runs when there wasn't so much as a taco truck for a hundred miles in any direction, this little getup had more than proven itself.

Setting up shop on the running board, Truck got his Julia Child hands screwed on and started cubing up Spam and dropping it into the skillet.

Say what you want about the sodium packed loaf of pink goodness, the aroma it kicks off on a hot griddle can rival any artisanal bacon on the market.

Evidently, he wasn't the only one who thought so, as Violet peeped like a groundhog through the open door, nose in the air.

"That's a fine way to wake up," she said.

"My way wasn't so bad either." He looked up at her as he beat water into the powdered eggs, letting the glimmer in his eyes tell her how little he minded waking with her in his arms. Evidently she saw it because she tucked her chin and blushed.

As much wild shit as he'd seen in the last day and a half, her flushed cheeks went a fair way to making up for it.

"This'll be ready in a second," he said as the slurry came together and the cubes of forcemeat crisped up.

"Thank you." When Truck only shrugged that it was fine,

her tone changed. "Hey." He looked up to find Violet regarding him steadily. "Thank you."

"Of course," he said without missing a stroke. "You're welcome." He might have said *my pleasure,* but they both knew that was some bullshit.

Violet pushed the door wider to slip down onto the ground, her long, pale legs shining in the sunlight. Clearly, she'd elected not to slip back into her jeans just yet, and Truck worked double time to keep his focus on the pan and not ogle her like some kind of trench-coated pervert.

As she glided over next to him, Truck got the very real feeling she wouldn't have minded if he did. The thought alone was enough to make his jeans tight, and he whisked around in the pan to keep from scooping her up for a repeat performance of the previous night's make out sesh.

"There's a thing of paper plates in the console," he said. "Plastic forks and stuff too."

"Just past all the new artillery," she smirked, and Truck raised an eyebrow at her.

"You disapprove?"

"Not at all." She left his side to hoist herself back up into the cab, looking back over her shoulder. "Anything is better than nothing."

"Damn right," he said, and she leaned over the seat.

The borrowed tee shirt rode up, revealing an ample view of her backside and the simple cotton panties she used to cover it.

"Damn right," Truck muttered again, prying his eyes away from the show he was pretty sure she was putting on for his benefit. Now that the cat of their mutual attraction was out of the bag, Truck had an even bigger stake in the whole thing.

And, every time she pulled a stunt like that, his personal stake got bigger.

Having breakfast wedged in a canyon might not be the most idyllic setting in the world, but after the wringer they'd been put through, any respite was welcome. Getting a bit of food in his belly did a lot to steady the gremlins crawling all over Truck's insides.

"Where are we, anyway?" Violet asked as she helped herself to another heaping forkful of the scramble.

"About sixty some miles out of Boone," Truck replied. "This is state owned property. Part of some sort of preserve or something. This particular nook is part of Valance Canyon."

Violet froze with her fork just in front of her lips. The way an animal freezes when it catches sight of the predator in the bushes.

"What?" Truck didn't have to ask, but he did anyway. He didn't need to be The Amazing goddamn Kreskin to know it was bad news.

"Like," Violet said faintly. "Exactly where?"

"There's a road map in the glove box."

Violet raccoon scrambled into the truck, not an ounce of the booty shaking she'd treated him to moments before. Reemerging in a flash, she thumbed through the atlas pages with shaking hands.

"I got it," he said, relieving her of it and opening the map to lay it out flat. "Okay, so..." Truck ran his fingertip along the access road line, looking for the turnoff he had taken to snug Layla into her little hideout. "Here," he pointed with certainty. "We're right here."

"Oh, no," Violet gasped just above a whisper. When Truck looked up to her face, he found she wasn't looking at the map at all. Her eyes were locked over his shoulder, gazing behind him to the far end of the rig.

EIGHT

Violet's heart balled up into a fist.

Sidling around from the back of the trailer was a figure she knew better than she would have liked. Everything in her blood told her to break into a dead sprint. For all the good it would have done.

The Chamberlain.

He wasn't in his Wolf, which in some ways made him more dangerous because he could be so easy to underestimate. Given Truck's stance as he got to his feet, underestimating was the last thing on his mind.

"If I were you, asshole," Truck said, "I'd turn back the way you came and start walking." His broad shoulders turned to iron as he faced the interloper, and Violet pressed her hands against them, tucking herself behind him.

"Truck," she whispered. "Don't."

The Chamberlain let a low, menacing chuckle and started a lazy stroll up along the side of the truck.

"Oh, my friend." He reached up and ran his fingernails along the scarred metal side as he walked. "You and I both know that's not how this is going to go."

"Figured I'd give you the chance," Truck said.

"You're confident." The Chamberlain twisted his lips into

a sardonic smile. "I like that. Almost as much as I like *this*." He pointed a knobby finger at Violet, waving it up and down to indicate her barely clad figure. The gesture alone would have been enough to curdle her guts, but the look in his eyes brought the acid sting of nausea to the back of her throat. "I've got to hand it to you, Vee. You really are something to see."

"Alright," Truck said with definitive finality. "That's enough of that."

Truck ignited the hotplate with a deft flick of his fingers, then took a few steps towards The Chamberlain to get the party started.

"Truck, please be careful," Violet whispered, and The Chamberlain tipped his head back to laugh in earnest, the cords in his scrawny neck sticking out.

"Wait." He clapped a hand on the side of the trailer, sending up a hollow boom as he continued to bray with laughter. "You mean to tell me this guy is called *Truck*? Like, *Truck* drives a goddamn *truck*? What a fucking—"

Before he could get out another word, Truck planted his fist square in The Chamberlain's jaw. The fucker let out a snorting grunt, the force of the blow snapping his head so far that it ricocheted off the side of the rig. A resonant clang went up, empty as the comfort it offered.

Not giving the son of a bitch a chance to recover, Truck heaved up with his left and caught The Chamberlain the ribs. The space between the rig and the rock face was so narrow that Truck's sinewy back obscured The Chamberlain's full reactions, but Violet could hear from the cringing rush of breath that he had clearly met with more than he bargained for.

"Violet," Truck called over his shoulder. "Get the shotgun."

She bolted into the driver's seat to lay hands on the weapon. Silver or not, a blast at this close range would leave

The Chamberlain in a bad enough way that it would take some legitimate time to put himself together again – so to speak.

The gun was heavier than she imagined, and Violet pulled herself slightly off balance as she dragged it up. Another series of meaty thuds from outside told her things were heating up, and she kicked the door open to get back out to try and head off the worst of it.

Just as she did, Truck crashed into it, The Chamberlain's arms wrapped around his waist. The Chamberlain's head was low by Truck's side, and it was clear he was trying to twist around to get his mouth on Truck.

"Don't let him bite you," she cried.

"Shut up, bitch," came The Chamberlain's muffled reply, but Truck's hand was in his hair before he could gain any purchase. Pulling back hard, Truck pried the filthy fucker's head out just enough to be able to look him dead in the eyes.

"You don't talk to her like that!" Darting his hand out, Truck grabbed the handle of the smoking pan on his hotplate and planted it on the side of The Chamberlain's face. He let out a terrible scream, and the immediate smell of sizzling flesh churned Violet's stomach.

The Chamberlain's grip slipped, and Truck shoved him back, peeling the red hot pan away, only to swing it down with impossible force. He did over and over again, and each part of exposed skin it kissed raised an ugly welt.

"Fuck this," The Chamberlain snarled, wresting himself backwards.

He disappeared from the doorway, and Violet leaned forward to look down the narrow corridor the men fought in. Truck moved to charge after The Chamberlain, but Violet planted a hand on his shoulder and clamped down hard to keep him in place. His muscles sang under her palm with the need for violence, and the vibration of it rattled the marrow of her bones.

"Don't," she hissed. Truck flashed a look up to her, but Violet kept her eyes locked on The Chamberlain's bristling, malice filled face.

He sneered with impossible fury, eyes yellowing as his breathing rasped out low growls. Saliva dripped from his gaping mouth, and his lower jaw elongated as more and more teeth crowded in. Bones popped as his arms contorted and his fingers stretched long.

"You're going to pay," The Chamberlain roared in a new, inhuman voice.

"Get in the truck," Violet pleaded. "We can go."

"No," The Chamberlain howled as the beast prepared to take over entirely. "You'll never escape your destiny!"

"Enough!" A new voice blistered the sky, shuddering over Violet with an icy blast. Truck looked up, and his face changed from one of fierce determination to a kind of fascinated awe. Violet didn't even have to lift her eyes to know who was gazing down on them.

"This is bullshit," The Chamberlain spat, still lingering halfway into his Wolf.

"I sent you down there for her," the voice overhead thundered. "Not for this. Violet?" The sound of her name on the man's lips made her quiver, and a feeling of hopelessness pooled in her guts like oil.

"Yes," she called back, still refusing to look up.

"The games are over. Come out now. You don't want to get that man killed."

"Violet?" Truck's voice immediately drew her eyes, and the sight of his face racked with concern wedged a glacier between her ribs. "Who is that?"

"The Duke."

Bringing herself to say even those words made her want to retch – there was no way she could elaborate without vomiting outright.

"Violet," The Duke's voice echoed again, this time thick with warning. "I won't ask again."

Trembling, Violet laid the shotgun back between the seats and braced herself to slide down. A numb tingling spread over her entire body, and she almost didn't feel the hand Truck put on the small of her back to help her down. He said something, but her ears were ringing too loud for her to make it out.

Worse, she was completely unable to meet his gaze. The terror looming over her was too great, and she had the miserable feeling that any hopes she had for her future had just come to an abrupt, brutal stop.

She fixed her gaze on The Chamberlain's malignant face, the smell of burnt dog hair stinging in her nose. He'd retreated to his human form as commanded, the savage burns on his skin glistening like raw meat.

Good. Serves you right, asshole.

She just wished Truck had had the good sense to smack the weasely fuck in the balls and burned them off with that pan. It would have eliminated at least one pressing danger.

Truck shifted aside to let her pass, catching hold of her upper arm.

"Violet," he whispered, but she was only able to raise her eyes to the center of his chest. "What's going on?"

"I need to face him," she replied. "I need him to see me."

It was enough of an answer for Truck to turn her loose, and he closed the door so she could slip by. As soon as the merciless desert sun pelted down on her back, the frozen sweat of her fear blasted to full, sticky life. When she was about fifteen feet in front of the truck, she turned and finally lifted her eyes to meet The Duke.

He stood on a bluff at the top of the canyon, maybe thirty feet above. Large as ever, his silvering hair blew in the breeze, his tattooed barrel chest heaving beneath his tattered leather vest.

"Well, well, well," he said, grinning as he looked her over. "Good to see you, Vee. Welcome home." Sticking his fingers in his mouth, the sturdy barbarian lashed out a piercing whistle, and a cacophony flooded the canyon until it seemed impossible the whole thing wouldn't fall in on itself from the noise.

The Pack teemed around a bend up the canyon like the goddamn Valkyries, every face alight with demonic joy at her capture. Violet stood with her shoulders squared in miserable resignation.

All at once, an arm snaked around her waist and she found herself pinned hard against the brawny frame of Truck Laine.

"Wait a goddamn minute," he shouted. "No way I'm letting this happen!"

"You don't have a choice, champ," The Duke called down from on high. "Whether you're alive, dead, or one of *our kind*," he said with fiendish relish, "Violet is coming with us."

"Then you're gonna have to work for it," Truck shouted, but Violet reached up a hand and placed it on his chest.

"Don't," she whispered.

He looked bewildered.

More than bewildered. Truck's face was utterly bereft. But as the cavalcade of jagged motorcycles encircled them in a tornado of rusted steel, it became clear The Duke had won the day.

A sudden wince of agony flashed across Truck's face. He arched backwards and his grip slackened. Only when The Chamberlain had her in his grip did Violet realize that the treacherous prick had taken a cheap shot at Truck's kidney.

"You're one lucky motherfucker," The Chamberlain jeered as he wrenched Violet away from Truck. "If it were up to me, you wouldn't have been given the option."

The Chamberlain smelled even worse up close, and the putrid stench of his festering wounds made Violet gag as he hauled her along. She stumbled trying to keep up, but despite his spindly frame, he was shockingly powerful.

As she knew only too well.

Dust choked the air, and Violet's mouth filled with so much grit it felt like her teeth would grind to nothing. The Chamberlain charged right into the center of the churning throng, dragging Violet like a felled deer. A chopper zipped close, and he snaked out an envious hand and collared the rider, yanking him from his saddle to land in the dirt with a horrible smack.

"What the fuck, man?" All that earned the protester was a boot in the teeth, and The Chamberlain strode away to commandeer the now vacant ride. It was one of the few with a sidecar, and he jammed Violet into it without the least regard. That done, he cast his leg over the top, kicked the pedal, and the hateful machine snarled to life.

As The Chamberlain brought the bike around, the clouds of desert soil parted just enough for Violet to catch sight of Truck standing sentinel in front of his rig.

"I'm sorry," she mouthed, and he was swallowed again by both the cloud, and the rabble kicking it up.

"Don't worry, Vee," The Chamberlain purred from beside her. "If you're looking for a lover boy, I know just the man." He stuck his fingers in her hair, rubbing his thumb along her jaw below her ear and leering down on her with possessive lust.

"After all," he chuckled. "I'm giving you a ride, the least you can do is return the favor."

NINE

The battalion of motorcycles obliterated the canyon floor, revving their engines until Truck thought his eardrums would pop.

But he refused to budge a foot.

Squinting into the swirling bedlam, he tried in vain to get eyes on Violet. No such luck.

This ragtag army of ghouls knew what they were doing, frothing up a literal smoke screen before vanishing around a bend. The air was almost too thick to breathe.

Not that Truck could anyway. His lungs were too full of concrete misery to make room for anything else.

He hadn't known Violet seventy two hours, but already losing her hollowed him out more than motel surgery. He might as well have been in a bathtub full of ice with a ragged, unfillable hole in his guts.

Nothing but Violet would plug it up again.

Casting his eyes up to the crag where the grizzled Biker King had stood, Truck found that he too had melted into the landscape. Another prairie phantom to haunt the rest of his days.

Truck had only gotten a brief glimpse of The Duke, but knew the exact measure of that kind of man. A tinpot tyrant who ruled through fear, brute strength, and sheer force of will. In his time, Truck had humbled scores of cocksuckers like that, and as long as he was this side of the dirt, he was ready to add one more notch to his belt.

"Fuck this," Truck spat, cracking his knuckles. "Not on my watch."

Charging around his rig, he clambered up between the cab and the trailer and started knocking connections free. Cables banged and slapped as one after the other swung loose, and before you can say Jack Spratt, he was at the crank dropping the support legs. There was no way he'd be able to pull the kind of shit he needed with the proverbial fifteen tons tied around his neck.

The trailer had to go.

"Sorry, lady," he said, laying a palm on the side of the war torn caboose. "I'll come back for you."

Back in the driver's seat, Truck readied himself for battle. Pistol on the dashboard, Pepper in the passenger seat, stock facing his hip. Easy access was key if he was going to bring the brand of ruckus he was after.

Am I really ready for this?

Stupid question.

Ready as I'm ever going to get.

Truck cranked the key and jammed his foot on the gas. Layla leapt forward like she'd been fired out of a canon. It wasn't the first time he'd driven his rig without her trailer – not by a longshot – but the sensation caught him in teeth every time.

All that power with nothing to pull basically turned the cab into a scud missile on land. Truck surged along the canyon floor like a pit bull in an orphanage. The Pack didn't have much of a head start, and Truck set his eyes on catching up before they could get out of the ravine and scatter into the desert.

The cab pitched with every bump in the dry riverbed,

chipping hunks from the sides of the canyon that would make an 1800s prospector blush. Out in the open he might have even flipped the goddamn thing, but the slalom kept him funneled into fiery pursuit. Sparks shot around his ears as Truck hugged his way around each bend in the narrow trail, but his iron focus stayed locked dead ahead.

The rock faces on either side shrank as Truck rose higher and higher towards level ground. The more blue sky that came into view, the more his eyes stung searching for the cloud of dust that band of brigands would be kicking up in their wake.

The instant he caught sight of it, Truck romped on the gas like it owed him alimony.

Just as sure as where there's smoke there's fire – where there was dust, there was Violet. Wherever that strangled knot of bikers was, she lay squarely at the beating heart of it, and Truck would be goddamned if he let them win on a technicality.

Layla grabbed air as Truck finally leapt out of the last bit of canyon, as gloriously happy to be out of the pinch as he was. Granted, she was the one getting banged and scraped by the stone walls, so maybe she had a little more reason.

"When all this is over," truck murmured, patting the dash, "I'm getting you a fresh coat of paint."

Now that he was out in the open, he had to keep his path as straight as possible. Rig cabs have notoriously high centers of gravity, and if he cut the wheel too hard he'd wind up rolling over. That wouldn't do anybody a lick of good.

Except maybe The Pack.

Too bad for them, Truck wasn't in the wish granting mood.

Aiming Layla's grill directly for the center of the hive, he shoved the gas pedal down so hard he damn near punched through the floorboard. The engine screamed louder than a stadium full of drunk soccer hooligans, and he closed fast on the herd of bikers. One of them must have spotted him because they fanned out and started to break around.

"Looks like a win to me," Truck muttered. With their ranks broken, he had a better shot of picking out the varmint who had Violet. Truck counted maybe three bikes with sidecars, and that narrowed down who he was after toot sweet.

Bracing his knee against the wheel, Truck fetched the shotgun and racked it against his chest. Then he rolled down both windows and it was time to party.

A handful of Pack members charged back at him, and one of their busted jalopies boasted a sidecar. The chances they were bringing Violet back wrapped in a bow were slimmer than eel shit, so this asshole was fair game. As they got closer, Truck squinted at the side car just to be sure, and was greeted by the ravening face of the monster he'd traded fisticuffs with on top of the rig.

"Scum," he muttered. "Come and get it."

They must have heard the invitation because they skidded close for some Ben Hur action. Before Truck could lean out the window to crack off a shot, Scum leapt from the side car onto his hood, claws furrowing gashes into the paint as he scrabbled to stay in place. That baleful wolfen face pressed so close to the windshield flecks of spittle spattered the glass.

An evil smile curled its lips, revealing even more cracked, yellow teeth. It reeled back a paw balled up into a sledgehammer fist, ready to punch a hole straight through the windshield and turn Truck's lights out.

"Not today." Truck jammed on the brakes and laughed out loud as Scum's eyes sprang wide and he flew backwards off the hood. The dumb fucker never saw it coming. No sooner had the brute cleared the hood ornament than Truck stomped the gas again, celebrating the thumping crunch as he ran Scum over like the garbage he was.

No silver, no dead Wolf, but crushing Scum's bones

would damn sure bench the fucker for a spell. The thought alone was enough for Truck to let out a triumphant whoop.

Unfortunately, the jollity was short-lived. A bullet whizzed past Truck's nose and popped a hole in the roof just over the passenger seat. On pure instinct his arm snapped out the window, and he pulled the trigger before he even turned his head to aim. Not that he needed to with Pepper doing the talking for him.

His eyes caught up with his hands just in time to see some furry face peel back off a skull. The beast pitched sideways with a gurgling shriek, taking his bike down in a crash for the record books. Fur, blood, shitty pants. The works.

Another rider was hot on that bastard's rear tire, and even if he didn't catch any of the pellets, there was no avoiding the aftermath. His bike slammed into the first and the lupine hellraiser shot over his handlebars to crunch down into the arid landscape.

"Two for the price of one," Truck smirked, but before he could pat himself on the back too hard, a terrible, grinding smack shook the passenger door. He whirled around just as it happened again, straining to glimpse not only of the culprit, but the scars he was leaving behind.

Someone's whipping me with a goddamn chain!

Truck reflex yanked the wheel to sideswipe whatever greasy prick was doing the whipping, and Layla all but pitched over. As he struggled to keep from going all tumbleweed, Truck gritted his teeth, shooting a tiny prayer to the man upstairs in hopes of keeping her upright.

It was so easy to forget he didn't have the five ton security blanket holding his tires down. Thankfully, the boss in the clouds was on his side for the moment, and Layla's wheels touched terra firma again.

A vindictive, snarling laugh gloated through the passenger window, chased by another punishing lash. Truck lifted his ass out of the seat and craned his neck to get a gander at who was to blame for all the bullshit, and even though the rider was Wolfed out, there was no mistaking The Duke.

Violet had said he never got his hands dirty, but Truck guessed it was filthy-paw o'clock.

Eyes blazing like cigar cherries in a rich man's ashtray, with a thick pelt of silver laced black fur, he and Truck looked directly into each other. The Duke's mouth hung open in a poisonous, fang crowded smile. His right arm shot over his head, swinging the chain in a vicious circle before letting it fly.

"Fuck this," Truck shouted as the metal bullwhip bit into Layla's side. Hoisting Pepper towards the passenger window just raised another evil laugh from the hulking monster. The Duke banked hard, peeling away to shoot off into oblivion, sending up a plume of stinking exhaust in his wake.

Missing out on dicking over the head Werewolf honcho dashed Truck's spirits, but he had other shit to attend to. Facing front again, Truck's eyes immediately locked on his target.

The whole hornet's nest was well and truly riled, but at the far head of the group was a chopper with a sidecar. The driver stole a furtive look back, but even at that distance Truck had no trouble recognizing the mane of red hair tossed by the wind from the buddy box.

It's her.

Now that he had eyes on Violet, nothing else mattered. He'd run over every last one of those Wolfman assholes who had the set of furry brass nuts to get in his way. If all that was left of his truck when he got to her was an axle and a steering wheel, so be it.

Dropping Pepper so he could lock his hands at ten and two, Truck set a literal collision course for The Chamberlain, swerving just a bit one way or the other as he carved his path. With each nudge of the wheel, some unholy asshole caught chrome. That should have been enough to let every creep in the Pack know that he didn't give a damn in hell about cleaning out as many as he could.

Without silver he may not be able to lay them down for the long haul, but he was more than content to put them out of commission for an hour or so.

As he chugged through the brambled thicket of screeching bikes, one hellish face after another glared at him. Each one was contorted in boiling hatred, and Truck more than returned the favor.

One rider got a little too close, and Truck grabbed his pistol off the dash and took a pot shot out the window. There was no telling whether it actually landed, but the leering dirtbag cleared out, which was the whole point.

The good news was he was gaining ground on Violet hard. The bad news was he was well and truly surrounded by The Pack. Even if he managed to get her back, it was going to be one hell of a fight to get clear of them.

Luckily for Truck, it looked like a fighting kind of day.

Judging by how The Chamberlain's shoulder glances ramped up in frequency, he had to know a showdown was coming his way. The only thing keeping Truck from running the bastard over outright was the woman in the sidecar. That precious cargo kept his raging blood in check.

For now, anyway.

Truck and Violet caught eyes, and that was all it took to send his heart hollering for more. This was the wildest caper he'd ever pulled, and as long as it ended up with her riding shotgun, it was worth every perilous second.

A thousand nights he'd laid in the dark whipping himself over the girl he couldn't save. Now that he was face to face with one he *could*, he'd be goddamned if he let her slip through his fingers.

Violet kept her gaze riveted to Truck's face, so terrified it made his bones ache. Whether for herself, or him – or both –

was a conversation to be had once she was safely strapped in next to him. Reassuring her with his eyes was nice and all, but there was only so much a confident look could do in the midst of a goddamn Werewolf tornado.

For his part, The Chamberlain was working overtime to keep directly in front of Truck. The son of a bitch had to know that there was no way under the blazing sun Truck would plow over him with Violet in the mix. And he sure as shit knew that if Truck got up alongside him, things would get real scrappy real quick.

The Chamberlain had already gotten a good taste of the business end of Truck's frying pan, so he knew what to expect.

Bad times and badder blood.

Layla's bumper all but dusted The Chamberlain's rear wheel, and every time Truck tried to move one way or the other the fucker headed him off. To make things worse, The Pack had gotten the drop on the situation and crowded around Truck fiercely.

Slobbering Werewolf faces were bad enough one at a time, and a whole throng of them baying for your blood was no Sunday picnic. If things didn't break Truck's way in a hurry, he might just find himself in trouble.

Even as he thought it, a hairy hand clamped down on the passenger side door. A monstrous face lunged in, snarling through snapping jaws.

"Not today," Truck shouted, striking out with his fist to clobber the swine right on the end of its snout. It blinked in startled agony, shooting up a clawed hand to cover its nose. That paw was all the grip it had, and the fucker clipped his chin on the window jamb as he fell out of sight.

"Time to clear a path," Truck said, grabbing Pepper again. Without so much as looking, he jabbed it out the driver's side window and kicked out a healthy round of random shots. Desperate, yelping squeals rang out, and Truck stretched over to offer the passenger side the same loving attention.

It damn sure thinned out the crowd, and Truck doubled down by jerking the wheel each way. Layla slued and rocked, but didn't go over. She did, on the other hand, give a lousy afternoon to whatever stupid scoundrels were riding close enough to taste her rubber.

That grabbed The Chamberlain's attention, and the craven chickenshit looked back in blind terror. The blatant cowardice was all the encouragement Truck needed, and he cut the wheel to the right to charge up alongside them. Caught off guard, The Chamberlain just sat in the saddle like a prize tit while Truck got himself into position.

He looked down from his window to see Violet staring up at him as the sidecar traded paint with Layla's running board. Just beside her, The Chamberlain howled and gnashed his fangs, the side of his face crusty with the burns Truck planted on him scabbing over.

"Duck," Truck shouted down at Violet.

"What?"

"Duck!"

She did as she was told, scrunching as low as possible to flatten herself against the top of the sidecar. The Chamberlain furrowed his brow in confusion, but only for an instant as Truck kicked his door open with all his might, cleaning the wolfish prick off his bike.

The bottom of the door only just cleared Violet's back, and she snapped her head up to find the driverless bike rapidly losing speed. Truck did his best to pace it, but without the weight of his trailer to balance things out, his rig started to bounce on a direct course to flipping like a bookie's quarter.

Truck shot his hand down, and Violet caught it immediately, her fingers tight around his forearm. She leapt hard as Truck pulled, soaring over his lap.

Just like the first time they met.

No sooner was she out of the sidecar than the chopper skittered off into a rolling tumble, sending parts spinning off into the mesquite brush never to be seen again.

Used to the game by now, Violet clambered across Truck and into the passenger seat while he slammed the door.

"You came for me," she said, breathless with wonder.

"Goddamn right," he replied. "If you think you can handle a shotgun, you might hang out your window and do a bit of housekeeping for me."

Violet grabbed the gun and racked it, ejecting a shell onto the dash.

"I grew up in the clutches of The Pack," she said. "I know my way around one of these."

"She'll want a reload." Truck thumped the dash and the glove box fell open, spilling buckshot as it did. Violet wasted no time feeding Pepper's hungry mouth, then turned to the window and got to blasting.

Nice as it would have been to admire her backside peeking out from under the shirt she had filched, Truck had other tasks at hand.

Grabbing the mic to his CB, he scrolled to Channel 33.

"Come on," he whispered. "Don't let me down." Raising the mic to his mouth, Truck called out into the static wilderness. "Break 33 for radio check, this is Hound looking for Fox. Fox, you out there? Over."

Silence.

"Goddamnit," Truck spat. "Come on, Dean."

"What are you doing?" Violet asked, taking a break from shelling to size up the situation.

"Taking a gamble," Truck said, then volleyed again. "Break 33, this is Hound. Fox, if you're out there, I need you, over."

Another snap and crackle of silence, and Truck's heart dropped. Regardless, he pointed Layla southwest and laid it on. Dean Harris was going to have company whether he liked it or not; it was just a question of whether he'd actually open the compound to let them in.

"Fox here," the radio hissed and Truck thumped his hand against the wheel in triumph. "What do you need, Hound?"

"An open door," Truck replied. "I'm calling in that favor."

TEN

"You've got to be fucking shitting me," Violet said as a barbed wire fortress came into view. "How the hell have I lived out here my whole life and not known about this?"

"That's Dean's whole thing," Truck said. "Not being known."

They drew closer, and Violet took in the magnitude of this sun baked citadel. A water tower anchored the front corner, doubling as a lookout spot. The walls were a formidable jumble of welded steel plates, barbed wire, oil drums, car parts, and god knows what else stretching over twenty feet into the air.

"That place looks absolutely impenetrable," she murmured.

"Yup." Truck nodded. "Dean built this thing to withstand an attack from just about anything." He looked at her, and the confidence in his gaze kindled a warm glow in her gut. "If we're gonna beat the devil, this is the place to do it."

Truck blared his horn as they rolled to a stop out front, and movement on the water tower arrested Violet's attention.

What she had assumed was an old tarp suddenly stood

up, a tangle of wild hair blowing above the wide, dark eyes of a pair of military grade binoculars. Truck jutted a hand out the window, and that seemed enough to satisfy their host. He spun around, hopped on a ladder, and whisked out of sight.

A sharp grinding sound went up a moment later, and one of the massive steel panels swung inward. Truck eased the rig through the narrow gate into the belly of this doomsday stronghold.

Violet peered down from her window as they rode in, finding a lanky, unshaven man looking back at her with suspicious, startlingly blue eyes. As soon as the back of the cab was through, the stranger heaved the door shut. It boomed across the plains with a resonant clang, and the man slid a massive steel beam into place, then set about turning keys on a whole array of locks.

Truck must have noticed the trepidation fluttering at the top of Violet's throat because he laid a hand on her thigh.

"Hey." He fetched Violet's gaze to his. "It's going to be okay. Dean's a friend."

She swallowed and nodded — not entirely convinced — as Truck cut the engine and opened his door. Life with The Pack had taught her to be wary of strangers. Or at least fearful *for* them. Being at Truck's side schooled her in another way of living.

Taking one last breath to steady herself, Violet followed his lead.

"How the hell are you doing?" Truck wore a large smile as he pumped Dean's hand. Even though Dean was smaller and spindlier than Truck, Violet didn't have a doubt in her mind that the wily little desert rat knew how to scrap.

"I'm alive," Dean replied. "That's what matters."

"You got that right," Truck agreed.

Again, Dean turned those ice blue eyes on Violet, and even though he didn't dip his gaze, she was suddenly very aware of how bare her legs were.

"Who's this?"

Does this guy ever blink?

"Dean, this is Violet," Truck said, his breezy tone doing little to settle her jittery guts. "She's the McGuffin to this whole tangle I've gotten myself into. Violet, this is Dean Harris. We grew up together."

"We became men together," Dean said in the weary breath of the battle battered damned. The queasy feelings racing around Violet's belly myst have been visible on her face, because Truck softened his voice and leaned in to explain.

"We were in Afghanistan."

"I see," she replied, as if she had any idea what that meant. Even if she had, something in the skittish sorrow that hung like a noose around Dean's neck told her there was more to the story.

"Yeah," Dean said in that same faraway tone. "Something like that."

Truck shifted uncomfortably and when his eyes flicked to Violet, there was an anxious glint in them she'd never seen before. And she'd seen plenty in their short time together.

The air was slick with secrets.

Not that she could begrudge it.

She had plenty of her own.

The fleeting reminder of all the darkness locked between her ribs sent a shudder over her, and she tried to banish the thought by scanning the inside of the enclosure.

"What is this place?" Her blatant astonishment was enough for Dean to crack his first smile, his reedy voice warming with pride.

"Paradise." He grinned. "Come on, I'll show you around." He and Truck fell in step, and Violet hesitated to look back at the improbably large steel gate. It was reinforced in every imaginable way – and a few she could never have imagined – but a nagging thought chewed at Violet's brain stem.

Is it enough?

"So," Dean said as they ambled along together. "What's the scoop? What drags you out to my little patch of dirt?"

"Get ready," Truck chuckled, stealing a glance back at Violet. Her guts shriveled like a worm on the sidewalk to think they had to lay out their whole situation to a man she didn't know the first thing about. Even so, Truck had opened the can. These beans were getting spilled one way or the other. "You ever heard of The Pack?"

"The Pack?" Dean snorted out a snide chuckle. "Every two bit operation out here dubs themselves some dumb shit like The Pack, or Warrior Station, or some wannabe badass thing. You're gonna have to be more specific." Truck stopped walking, put his hands on his hips, and the three of them circled the wagons. Every molecule in Violet violet's body seethed and tingled.

Here it is. The moment of truth.

"First time I laid eyes on Violet," Truck began, gesturing to her with his elbow. "She was running full tilt boogie down the center of the interstate. And hot on her heels was a straight-up army of bikers." Dean's eyes sprang wide, and Violet silently begged the earth to open up and swallow her down to hell.

"No shit," Dean mumbled.

"It gets better." Truck shook his head, staring at the ground with a bemused smile. "Dean, I don't know any other way to say this, so I'm just gonna have to do it." He lifted his gaze and looked his friend right in the eye. "They're Werewolves."

A whole symphony of shit washed over Dean's narrow face. Disbelief, laughter, confusion, incredulity, bewilderment, insanity. The whole shooting match. In the end, he ground his fingers in his eyes and pinched the bridge of his nose.

"Wait. Hang on a second." He put out both hands as if to

steady the air around them, and looked Truck full in the face. "You're telling me you rescued this gal from a gang of motorcycle riding Werewolves?"

"That's about the size of it," Truck replied.

Dean huffed out a laugh, gave Truck a dangerous sideways look, then tipped his head back to look at the cloudless sky as he gnawed on his bottom lip. After a second, he nodded and looked at Violet again. She got the very real feeling he was appraising her. Weighing up how much to believe, and whether she was worth stepping through the wardrobe for.

"Alright, fuck it," he said. "I'm in."

And that was that. In the flash of an instant, he accepted that Werewolves were real, and the three of them were going to face them down together.

Violet's heart soared. She could never have conceived a friendship like this. Truck had brought chaos into his buddy's cast iron world, and the guy had swallowed it whole and held out his plate for seconds.

She'd lived her entire life under the hopeless truth that she was locked into a hateful, inescapable fate. The kind that brought a bloody eternity she loathed to her core. Now, with the help of these two men, it seemed possible that she might be able to break free.

If they could just manage to kill The Duke within the next three days, a whole new world would open up for her.

~

"I gotta hand it to you, Dean," Truck said as they toured the enclosure. "If the shit ever goes down, you'll be more than ready."

"Oh, it'll go down," Dean replied with a grim certainty that lodged like a stone in Violet's chest. "The day is coming fast."

He's got no idea how right he is.

"Anyhow." Dean shrugged off the darkness, and a dash of pride set the Adam's apple bobbing in his throat. "The water tower is good for a half million gallons or so, and I've got enough MREs to keep me on my feet for the rest of my natural life even if they dropped the bomb tomorrow."

"Impressive," Violet said, trying to match their ready camaraderie. Dean turned to give her that sideways smile of his, quickly giving way to a look of pure shock.

"You're not wearing any pants," he shouted, registering the way she was dressed for the first time. Squirmy as it made her, it felt good to know he hadn't been secretly ogling her since her arrival.

"Um..." Violet shifted uneasily from foot to foot, but the guy took off across the yard like a ferret.

"You two follow me," he called over his shoulder. She and Truck fell in step, arriving at a sizable outbuilding just as Dean was sifting through a hula-hoop sized key ring. "Here we go." Dean held up a key, knocked off the padlock, and led them inside.

"Holy shit," Violet gulped as soon as they crossed the threshold.

Floor to ceiling weapons stared back at her, each one oiled up and ready for action. Long guns, assault rifles, sawed off blasters, pistols of every stripe and size. Mountains of ammo boxes arranged in blocks to make tables, and Violet knew without asking that each and every one was full to capacity.

Dean hunkered down next to one and started tossing through a cardboard box full of stuff. As he rifled away, Violet inhaled the familiar aroma of gun oil and powder. This wasn't just an armory – it was a workshop.

As if drawn by a magnet, she crossed the space to stand next to Dean's master station. It stood more than equipped to manufacture ammunition for just about every musket in the joint.

"Here," Dean said, stepping up beside her. "These are the

smallest I got." He held out a pair of olive drab military issue trousers and even though the canvas was rough to the touch, she was grateful for anything that wasn't her tattered, sweat-smoothed jeans.

"Thank you." Unexpected tears welled up to choke her voice. The generosity of strangers was foreign territory to her, and she was afraid of getting too comfortable with it.

"Woah, hey!" Seeing water in her eyes, Dean backed away like she was an active bomb. "Did I do something wrong?"

"No," she chuckled softly, swabbing her cheeks. "It's just —" Words came up short, so she reached out and embraced the wiry prepper. He seemed startled at first, but after a bare moment, he wrapped his arms around her in return.

"It's alright," he said. "Anybody running with Tucker here is welcome to whatever I got."

"Thank you," she repeated as she let him go, wiping her nose on her shoulder as she shook the pants out to step into them. When she did, Violet's eyes flicked to find Truck watching her like a dog on a leash. Evidently Dean saw it too because he cleared his throat and sidled towards the door.

"Come on," he said. "I'll show you guys your room." He rapped the door jamb and walked back out into the baking sun, leaving Violet and Truck in the cool dim of the arsenal.

"*Our* room?" She raised an eyebrow, and Truck just shrugged.

"I'm sure he's got plenty of bedrooms in this place if you feel like having one of your own."

"No," she said immediately. "No, I think Dean is right on the money."

ELEVEN

"How are you?" Violet flinched at the sound of Truck's voice.

He watched her with his arm up on the doorway, and she visibly melted at the sight of him. The ramrod in the front of his jeans already ached from being hard all goddamn day, but the look in her eyes made him swell even more.

"I think I'm okay." She sighed, but Truck could tell by the way as she fidgeted with the waistband of her bulky trousers that she was putting on a brave face. "I just can't help thinking..." She trailed off, but Truck finished for her.

"They're still out there."

Violet looked at him, her face as open as a Black Friday Best Buy, and every bit as fearful. She gave the tiniest nod, and Truck's insides buzzed like a kicked hornet's nest.

"Look," he said, coming closer to where she sat on the corner of the bed. "You've seen this place. They may be out there, but it would take an atomic blast to get them in here."

"Maybe." She clearly wasn't convinced.

"Okay." Truck thumped onto the mattress next to her and laid a hand on her thigh. The coarse fabric was a far cry from her smooth skin, and he had to stifle how much he missed it. "I know there's a lot you're not exactly itching to talk about, but you're gonna have to let me in on *some* of it. Like, why are you so sure they're going to find us here?"

"Me," she said softly. "They're going to find *me*. If it was just you, they'd never get within twenty miles of this place."

"Why?" He stroked his thumb across her leg, and she started to tremble.

"Because." Violet lifted her eyes to him, and Truck almost fell head first into the chasm of worry and shame just behind her pupils. "They know my scent," she said at last. "I don't even know what I was thinking running off in the first place. I was just..." A heavy sigh fell into her lap. "Out of options."

"How long were you with them?" he asked. "I know I've asked before, but just how long does it take to learn a person's scent?" She clenched her jaw, staring at the bare concrete pad as if the answer was chiseled there.

"They'd know me anywhere." The enigmatic answer didn't do a damn thing to satisfy Truck, so he watched and waited.

"How long?"

"Years," she blurted in a ragged confession. "My whole life. I was raised in The Pack, okay?" She wheeled on him, eyes red with tears, jaw jutted out in defiance. "Is that what you wanted to hear?"

"I'm not trying to pry—"

"Then don't," she cut him off, and the back of Truck's throat went all acidy. "I'm not grilling you for answers, am I?"

"Well, I'm not the one who was on the lam from a bunch of goddamn Werewolves." It was a shitty thing to say, and it was clear from Violet's eyes she took it shittily.

"Maybe," she bit back, "but you sure are thick with some balls-out doomsday prepper. Maybe I should be asking you how you got chummy enough with him to get us into this bear trap." The words stung Truck's temper and he spoke without thinking.

"I saved his life, okay?"

He hated saying shit like that, but the words tripped out of him like a boxcar wino. In any event, the confession caught her up because all the defensive bitterness vanished from her face.

"What?"

"Look, it's not a big deal." He tried to shrug it off. "Forget I said it." Now it was his turn to stare at the floor, his chest burning with the memory.

"Truck," Violet said, her voice timid as a field mouse. "Tucker?" The sound of his true name on her lips drew him back, and when he faced her again she was all softness and care. "What happened? Was it in the war?"

"It was after." An odd croak in his throat surprised him, and he tried to hide it behind a laugh. "Shit, all we did in Afghanistan was drive jeeps around and shoot at soda cans. We did one tour, then came back to the states to get back to real life. Whatever that means." He shook his head and stared off into space for a second, wondering how twenty-one year old Truck would have reacted to know that 'real life' had fucking Werewolves in it.

"And?"

Something about her was irresistible, and while he'd spent years letting Dr. Interstate act as his therapist, it was clear Violet was going to worm her way in. What startled Truck even more was the fact that he *wanted* to let her in. Opening up wasn't his strong suit, but this girl made him want to take lessons.

Heaving in a weighty breath, Truck got ready to roll away the stone.

"When we got back from Afghanistan, Dean and I were basically Good Time Charlies for a bit. No jobs worth a damn, burning youth at both ends and trying to figure out what the hell to do with the rest of our lives. That kind of thing. Just running around like a couple of dumbasses."

"Sounds nice," Violet said, and Truck had to consider that if she'd grown up around The Pack, she'd likely never had a single day like that.

"It was," Truck admitted. "For a while. Anyway, Dean wound up dating my sister, and the three of us tore ass all over our little patch of West Texas. So, one night..." A jagged lump set up shop square in the middle of his throat, and no matter how hard Truck swallowed, he couldn't dislodge the wicked fucker. The cords in his neck went hot and tight, and he clicked his tongue against his teeth. "One night..."

"You don't have to," Violet said suddenly. "I'm sorry I asked."

"No." Truck shook his head and patted her leg. "No, I should get it out." Folding his fingers in his lap, he stared through the floor right down to the bomb shelter under their feet, and let his story fall into the open.

"One night we were out drag racing each other on a dirt road. I had this little blue Camaro I thought was hot shit, and Dean had this black pickup that had hit just about everything but the lottery. Anyhow, Jenn was riding with him, and I had a healthy lead. And, as you can imagine," Truck shrugged to indicate the compound around them, "Dean doesn't do anything halfway. So me being ahead wasn't gonna wash, especially in front of my sister. He stomps on it, and they zoom up quick. But, before they can break ahead, he blows a tire and starts fishtailing all to hell. Then it jerked sideways and the damn thing rolled."

"Oh, God," Violet murmured, her hand shooting up to her mouth. Truck could tell she knew exactly where this was headed, but he forced himself to keep going.

"Jenny got thrown clean out the window. I don't know whether the truck rolled twice or five times, but sometimes when I think about it, it seems like it just kept flipping forever. I don't remember turning around, stopping the Camaro—none of it. All I know is I was crouching down in the brush trying to hold the back of Jenny's head together. I was saying all the comforting shit I could, but it didn't matter. The lights were already out."

"Truck." It was barely a whisper, and he took her hand, lacing their fingers together. It felt good, and before long he was hanging on like she was the only thing keeping him from sailing off into the sky.

"Anyway," he trudged ahead. "I hear this hollering, and when I look over, Dean is upside down in that goddamn farm truck. The roof's caved in, and he's stuck real good. And while I'm sitting there holding my sister, the fucking thing catches fire. And I told myself I wasn't gonna lose both of them in one night, so I went over and pulled him out. Cut the seatbelt with my knife and got him out of there."

A fog of quiet frosted the air, and they sat side by side on the bed, Truck absently squeezing her fingers in a steady heartbeat rhythm. He'd never spoken about the accident to anybody outside the family, but he'd watched it replayed countless times as he let the white lines zipping by lull him into numbness.

"You know the funny thing?" Truck turned to look into Violet's wide, liquid eyes. "It's like Dean couldn't forgive me for pulling him out. The second he could re-enlist, he was off again, and the next time I set eyes on him, he was the kind of guy who does this." Again, Truck nodded at the whole compound.

Silence shoved into the room and wrapped the duo in its chilly embrace, drinking the misery dry.

"Truck," Violet said softly after a long pause. "I don't know what to say."

"You don't have to say anything." He shrugged, pulling his lips into a tight line to keep them from trembling. "Thanks for listening." He wasn't sure if he felt better, but at least the demons were standing on the outside of his skull instead of clawing at the inside.

Violet scooted closer and laid her head on his shoulder, and it just felt so *right*. The weight of her head, and the way it fit so easily in the hollow of his neck. Her tapered fingers intertwined with his. By all rights they should have been smooth and tender, but they were just like his – calloused, rough, and uncompromising.

His breath came in thick, the way it does when your chest knows what's coming. When your breathing synchronizes with the person you're next to, and your skin comes alive in that glistening way that says – *we both want this*. And there's no denying it.

"Violet," he whispered, voice husky.

"Yes?"

"May I kiss you?"

She didn't say yes. Merely tipped her chin up, and he turned his head, and their lips found each other like destiny.

TWELVE

Ever since their first hot-and-heavy make out session, Violet's insides *begged* for this. An insatiable gremlin in her heart demanded a passionate, lawless, untamable tangle – but this was different.

Truck had just shared something more than his brawn and inexplicable determination to protect her at any costs. This wrought iron hero had a vulnerable core so unfathomable it made her knees knock.

His desperate need to protect her wasn't so inexplicable after all.

It was as clear as the midnight sky that he needed someone to keep safe. Someone he could pour all of his battered heart into.

Someone whose life he could save.

Maybe, just maybe, that someone could be her.

She slipped her hand from his and let it wander up along the firm planes of his chest. Every sculpted inch chased her scorching breath higher in her lungs. If she kept touching him like this, she was bound to pass out, but she couldn't stop if she wanted to.

And she damn sure didn't want to.

Truck's own hammering heartbeat played on her

fingertips, telling her she wasn't in this party all by herself. His impossibly sinewy body responded like fire to her touch, stoking her hunger to the point of insanity.

"God," he murmured into her ear, his lips abandoning her mouth to glide along the line of her jaw. "Violet, you're so fucking *perfect*." The gentle scrape of his stubble left her panting just as much as the words riding his husky breath. She groped up to his neck and fastened her hand there, pulling him closer.

Whatever madness he let loose in her blood, she was starving for as much as she could get.

Truck read her like a dimestore novel.

The subtle exploration of their kiss melted in the crucible of their passion, and in the space of a heartbeat, her core flooded with molten need. Gulping in huge breaths, each one escaped in a low moan as the man in her arms ministered to her every secret desire.

These were fantasies she kept under lock and key for fear of igniting a bonfire she'd never be able to put out. Who knows what would happen if any of The Pack had caught her trying?

But now she was hidden away with the only person in the world she could trust. Which meant she could finally let her naughtiest self off her leash.

The skin she'd fought so hard to deny came roaring to life, crackling with magnetic sensitivity to Truck's every touch. The lightest brush sizzled like a match strike. If things kept on like this, they'd burn the whole compound down.

Violet was perilously close to dissolving into liquid pleasure any instant. His hand stalked up her thigh towards her hip with firm, delectable slowness. As if the butter of his lust rode on the underside of his palm to slather over her hungry, waiting skin.

Dean's generosity suddenly made her furious. If he hadn't

given her this pair of bulky trousers, Truck's hand would be directly on her body.

Where it belongs.

The thought alone set off a tiny explosion in her core, and a slippery tingling unlike anything she knew before bloomed like a desert flower between her thighs.

"Fuck," she gasped, gripping him hard.

"Are you alright?" Truck's lips hung frozen just at the dip above her clavicle, warm, whispered breath fogging over her skin. "Violet?"

Words failed. Violet pulled him to her, the delirious humidity of his mouth rendering her dumb to anything but pleasure. The Duke, The Chamberlain, Scum – the whole Pack vaporized in an instant. There was nobody under God's sky but Violet and the powerful, sensitive man lavishing her with decadent sensuality.

His fingers dug into her hip and Violet rolled on top of him as if pulled by invisible strings. She straddled him so easily she swore they had been crafted to fit together. Truck's hand anchored on the small of her back while the other climbed up the rollercoaster of her spine to find the crest between her shoulder blades.

Then his hips slid up to press into her and sparks shot under her skin.

"Fuck," she hissed again, digging her fingers into his hair. How was it possible to feel so lost and so secure all at once?

Taking on a life of their own, her hips rocked to meet him, and the massive, rigid bulge in his jeans nudged against her again. An atomic blast detonated in her pelvis. All her breath rushed out, and she clenched him against her so tightly she was afraid she'd suffocate him. The fear of it was useless against the merciless, grinding devil in her core.

"Um…" she whimpered as her legs began to quiver. "Truck?" He kissed her neck harder, the scrape of his cheeks rubbing her skin red. An unstoppable force spooled up inside her so that her legs locked, the joints of her hips itching with urgent insanity.

I can't move again. If I move again, I'll never stop.

She moved again.

Just the tiniest, timid wisp of gyration. And she shattered into pieces. Every particle of her burst into a star, pulsing with cosmic fire. She scratched at his shirt and riveted her knees to him, while his strong hands kept her from spinning off into the universe.

Everything fell apart until she was lost in herself. Tossed on a blinding sea that left her begging to drown.

"It's alright," he murmured when her brain started to coalesce inside her skull again. "It's alright, I've got you."

God.

How was his voice so *soothing*? It might as well have been coming from inside her own chest.

"It's alright," he repeated. That broad, powerful hand rode down her back in long, leisurely swipes, and her breath juddered back into her like a foreign thing.

And then she realized she was crying.

"I'm sorry," she said, covering her face with a hand and blushing at herself. "I don't know what's wrong with me."

"Hey." Truck nuzzled at the back of her hand until she let it fall, and his rich, hypnotic eyes awaited her. "There's nothing wrong with you. Nothing. Do you hear me? And you don't ever have to be sorry for anything ever again." He kissed the tears on her cheeks, which only made her drop more for him to catch.

Once her tears stopped, Truck shifted so that Violet could slide out of his lap onto the bed.

The immediate loss of his heat made her shiver – especially how cold her nether regions felt now that her underwear was soaked. She lay back like a loose jointed doll, reeling from the powerful climax she'd just weathered. After a beat, Truck stood and sauntered to the door.

"You're not leaving?" she asked, shooting up to her elbows in panic. Truck turned back to her with a playful smirk.

"Is that what you think?"

Without taking his gaze from her face, he reached out and shut the door. The finality of the knob clicking into place made her weak as a dying breath. Truck crossed back to the bed with measured steps, his voracious eyes making a meal of her spread out before him.

First, he kicked off his boots, then stripped his tee shirt over his head and tossed it aside. Violet knew what his body felt like under her hands, but actually seeing it was something else altogether.

This man had to spend every second he wasn't behind the wheel lifting that goddamn truck over his head. The son of a bitch must've been sculpted by the hand of Zeus himself.

Shit, even his muscles had muscles.

When his fingers tugged at his belt, Violet balled up the sheets in her fists. White hot anticipation bubbled in her blood. His button fly jeans fell open with an abrupt snap, and as Truck slid them down, Violet got her first glimpse at the Goliath in his boxers. She'd ridden up against it just moments before, but now the merest glimpse of what he was packing blew her eyelids back in astonishment.

When Truck slid his boxers all the way down, she damn near passed out. A convulsion stole over her with such conviction she almost came again on the spot. Sure, she'd seen members of The Pack naked, their floppy, smudgy pricks inspiring vomitous shame.

But this was a *man*. For the first time, she saw what the real deal was supposed to look like.

And there was no question Truck was swinging the real deal.

He eased onto the bed, and a reverberating echo in her core hummed to life. He was so close, and he was *so* naked.

"Is this alright?" he whispered as he spread himself beside her, kissing her shoulder. Violet's breath slammed her throat shut, so all she could do was nod. "How about this?" He plucked at the bottom of the tee shirt she had staked her claim to, lifting it just enough so that his rough fingertips could brush on the soft plane of her belly.

She gripped the sheets even tighter, eyes rolling as a blissful prickle etched over her. He lifted the shirt higher until it rumpled around the underside of her ribs. Truck poised himself over her, planting a kiss on her stomach. The kiss deepened as he sank lower, delving just the tip of his tongue into her navel. A sizzling bolt of flame licked along Violet's spine, and she arched her back and cried out.

"Oh, my God!"

Unable to bear the delicious torture of Truck's lingering touch, Violet's hasty hands leapt up and snatched off the shirt in a single swipe. There she was, the whole of her torso open to his gaze, and Truck's face dimpled with adoration as he drank in the sight of her body. The radiant tenderness made her tremble, and her chest tightened as he dipped his head low to taste her nipple.

"Shit," she murmured as his warm, wet mouth closed around her, the flicking pressure of his tongue drawing her up to shimmering rigidity. When he took the point lightly between his teeth and teased her, a dam burst in her stomach, and Violet was swept off in the torrent.

"Am I hurting you?" Truck asked, her nipple still nestled between his teeth.

"Keep going," she pleaded. "For God's sake, don't stop." Truck did exactly as he was told. At the same time, his hand worked at the button to her trousers, and as he eased the zipper down, the pressure of his touch on her mound sparked a fresh array of goosebumps.

Suddenly, his mouth was gone, and a pained breath swooped into her chest like a knot of sparrows.

"Don't," she cried, reaching out for him with chilled, desperate fingers. "Don't stop!"

Truck sat on the edge of the bed, that same lazy half smile painting his face.

"Don't worry," he said. "I'll be right back."

Taking the belt loops of her trousers, he released her from them with near reverence.

Then, he tucked his fingers just beneath the waistline of her panties, looking at her sideways by way of asking permission. Violet bit her lip and nodded, and as Truck's touch grazed down along her legs with the flimsy cotton in tow, that treacherous glistening between her thighs glowed to life again.

Violet let her legs fall wide, unashamed for the first time in her life. Truck ran his hands from her knees up along the inside of her thighs, fretting along the joints of her hips, soothing her sides up to her ribs, and soon her body was covered with his.

Violet offered her lips, and Truck met them as a rare delicacy. Sweet and lingering, his fingers slipped into her hair to cradle the back of her head. She pressed herself up to meet him, eager to feel as much of his body as possible. Sliding one hand between them, shock washed over her again as she wrapped her hand around his cock.

Fuck. There's just so much of it.

It was hot and hard, tensing in her hand like a python. Lost to anything but the dizzying need for him, Violet brought Truck to her, parting herself to welcome him.

Truck's crown eased past her entrance, and her hands rocketed to his ass as a feverish war broke out inside her. She yearned to pull him in all at once, while at the same time, begging him to take her slowly. Furious as her need was, if he surged inside in one thrust, she knew she'd die.

"Please," she mouthed, breathless. "Go slow."

"God," he mumbled, coming so close his hot breath flooded her ear. "With pleasure."

And he pushed.

A deliberate, merciless march so more and more of him swelled in to fill her. It was devastating. A billion bursts of pleasure rode just up to the border of pain as he seemed to sink into her forever. The head of his cock chased her breath higher and higher into her chest, that mad gyroscope in her blood spinning to the tipping point.

Just when it seemed like she might start screaming and never stop until the world collapsed, his hips came to rest against the underside of her legs. She drank in air in short, percussive gulps, her hands fluttering over his body unable to find a place to land.

One of his palms still cradled her head, and his other pressed along the mattress to find the small of her back. Once there, she was wholly embraced – enfolded into this man whose body shielded her from everything while piercing her to the very center at the same time.

Then he rocked his hips.

Pushing deep, then drawing back just enough for her to pine for the loss of him. With each roll, his hip bone ground against her clit until her brains melted out her ears onto the pillows. It was a ravishment, and her body answered his on pure instinct. Their rhythms aligned, and soon she was grunting as she bucked up to meet him.

The animal in her threatened to take over, and her tenuous grasp on its chain both terrified her and ignited her carnal insanity all at once. Violet's backbone arced and bent, driving herself into him as she chased the biggest dragon in creation.

"Fuck," she snarled as she kicked her heels at the ceiling. "Fuck, fuck fuck," over and over again in a rising crescendo as Truck's hips piled down into her with ruthless abandon.

Her insides were like a fiddle string ready to snap, and

with each passing second, the break became more and more inevitable.

"Truck..." Words lost meaning as her whole body began to convulse.

"Shit, Violet, I'm gonna come."

That was all it took.

A thunderbolt ripped her body in half, and she howled out as the swirl utterly consumed her. Truck's fervent burst in her core tossed her deeper into the whirlpool, robbing her of anything but ecstasy. Her little boat struggled in the waves, and each time he throbbed, spilling more of himself to fill her, she guttered again and threatened to go under.

"Fuck, Violet," Truck growled through gritted teeth, and she latched her arms around him so they could weather the gale together. Passion spun them up in each other so tight there was no chance of separating again. Not after this.

Their bodies slackened together, hearts pounding in exact time. The drum of his answered her through his chest, lulling Violet to numb, sublime calm. Rivulets of sweat ran over her skin, reminding her that she had a body after all. She was more than a white hot bundle of staggering bliss.

As their breaths subsided and the real world began to crowd back into the corners of the room, Violet held Truck and tried to memorize every morsel of him.

Be careful, she cautioned herself.

I'm in serious danger of falling in love with this guy.

THIRTEEN

Truck's eyes blasted open, panic splintering his nerves. *What time is it? Where am I?*

Dean's rabbit warren of rooms and hallways was big on security, short on windows. Truck might as well have been buried underground, and if he was the claustrophobic type he'd have ripped the walls down with his bare hands.

Fortunately for Dean's handiwork, having Violet curled up beside him sure as hell knocked the edge off things. The steady rhythm of her breath said she was conked out, and Truck did his best to slip out of bed without ruffling any feathers. After the night they'd had, she probably needed the sleep.

Fumbling back into his clothes in the dark, Truck ducked through the door as quietly as he could and prodded his way down the dimly lit corridor. The smell of coffee wafted out to him, and he damn near floated down the hall on the aroma.

"Look who's up," Dean smirked over his cup. "I'm amazed to see either one of you. Figured you'd be in that room for the next calendar year."

"Tempting, but..." Truck trailed off, letting the implication hang as he splashed out a gout of joe so thick it might as well have been tar. "Hope we didn't keep you up?" Dean just shrugged and took another long sip.

"Listen." Dean put down his mug and slid it away from him with his thumbs. He didn't lift his eyes, and Truck could tell the wiry cuss had something on his mind. "A tumble's fun and all, but how much do you really know about this girl?" It was a ballsy question, and if it had been anyone else, Truck's first impulse might just have been to clean his clock. But Dean was the closest thing Truck had to a brother, which his raw dog honest question deserved an honest answer.

"I'm going to level with you—not much."

"Yeah." Dean pulled his lips tight and inhaled sharply through his nose. "That's kinda what I thought." Slumping back in his seat, he looked up to meet Truck's eyes. "Man, Werewolves? You're in pretty goddamn deep for a girl you don't know spit about. You sure this is the move?"

"I've wondered that myself." The problem had slithered in Truck's belly like a serpent from the minute he laid eyes on Violet. No matter what angle he looked at it, he always found himself in the same set of shoes. "I have to tell you, Dean—this girl needs help, and I can't just pull a catch and release on this one."

"Maybe." Dean nodded a second, then sighed hard. "Truck, you're not gonna like this, but I've got to say it. She's not being straight with you." He said it so plainly it damn near knocked the flaking paint off the walls. "She's got a secret she's not diming out, and you can see it all over her face."

"We've all got secrets," Truck countered, wishing like hell he could shut this conversation down.

"Sure," Dean conceded. "But not all of them grow fangs under the full moon." Truck bristled, and Dean must have seen it because he tilted his head to the side and drummed his fingers on the tabletop. "I'm just saying be careful is all. I mean, how long was she even with The Gang or whatever?"

"Her whole life," Truck said, and as soon as the words were out a cold smear of discomfort slicked up his spine. Dean huffed a laugh through his nose.

"Ain't that something?" He slid his cup close again and gazed down into it for a second. "Girl like that spends her whole life with Werewolves? Makes a fella wonder."

Dean took a sip while the treacherous implications leaked all over Truck's guts. His buddy was asking the questions Truck had purposely kept himself blind to, and his neck got hot as he tried to stuff Pandora's plagues back into her box.

"One thing you should know," Truck said, doing what he could to push back the clouds and get his brain back on track. "It's not just the full moon with these fuckers. They can get all hairy pretty much at will."

"Of course," Dean chuckled at the absurdity of it all. "Why the hell not? Keeps things interesting. What about the whole silver thing? Is that still good, or do you need uranium or something?"

"Evidently silver is what we're after," Truck said. "Which brings up another question—I hate to ask, but...?"

Dean clapped his cup down like a hammer and scrubbed his face with both hands. Running them up into his bramble of hair, he cut his eyes up to Truck, and Truck could tell his lifelong friend didn't like where this was heading.

"Yeah," Dean said at last. "I got some. Come on." Shoving up from the table, Dean shook his head and squeaked in a breath through his teeth. The son of a bitch was clearly miffed, leading Truck out into the yard without so much as looking back. It was morning, but the day was already hotter than the devil's nutsack, and Truck all the was stickier for it.

"Look," Dean grunted as he fingered through his omnipresent key ring. "Don't get all hog wild when we go into this place. Building up a bank like this ain't easy, and it damn sure wasn't cheap."

"None of this was cheap," Truck grinned, nodding in admiration at the entire compound.

"Goddamn right." The pride on Dean's face chipped away some of his sourpuss attitude, and he clicked the padlock open. "I'm happy to help you out if you need it, but once we start dipping into this?" He rapped on the steel door with his knuckle. "It ain't free. I'm gonna need you to pay me back."

"I wouldn't have it any other way," Truck swore. "I'm not here to take advantages."

"I know you're not, buddy." Suddenly mournful, Dean reached out and put a hand on Truck's shoulder. "Sorry. It's just—as soon as folks know you got shit, everybody wants a piece of the pie. I got pretty goddamn tired of folks showing up with a billion watt smile and empty hands."

"I promise." Truck kept his gaze steady so his friend would know how sincere he was. "I'll pay you back. I'll make it all good." A midnight phantom stole across Dean's face, and he aged seventy years in an instant.

"Nobody can make it *all* good," he said wearily as he pried the door open. "And you already paid plenty." He stepped across the threshold and flicked on the light, tromping down a spiral staircase into a vault. When Truck followed, his mouth fell open wide enough to catch every fly in the desert.

"You've got to be fucking kidding me."

"Not bad, huh?" Dean's mischievous smile returned, and he put his hands on his hips as Truck took it all in. "Willy Wonka ain't got shit on me."

The armory was one thing, but this treasure pit would have made King Midas' dick hard. Storybook dragons would blush in envy at the heap of glittering loot crowded into this unassuming outbuilding.

Nail kegs stood heaped with gemstones, one crowned with a diamond the size of a strawberry. Pallets of gold ingots held down the center of the room, flanked by smaller mountains of silver. Crowded around on shelves were basins, and ewers, and idols, and samovars, and tangles of beads and chains all made from precious metals.

"Sorry about the mess," Dean said, waving lazily at a heap of pitchers and candlesticks on one shelf. "This is all the stuff I haven't gotten around to melting down yet. Usually do that in the fall or winter."

"How the hell?" Truck caught himself and put his hands up. "You know what? Nope. I'm not even going to ask."

"Just time," Dean said enigmatically. "Time and money. Maybe a little bit of sneaky thinking. Anyway, let's get to it." He picked up two silver bars each about the size of a deck of cards and tossed one to Truck. When he caught it, Truck was so startled he damn near dropped it.

"Are you kidding?" he asked, eyes wide. "That thing's gotta weigh two pounds!"

"Close," Dean raised an eyebrow as he picked up another one. "One kilo." He shouldered past Truck and out into the yard again. "What caliber bullet do you want? And how many rounds are we talking?"

"Shotgun shells to start," Truck said. "Keep it simple, and cover the most ground."

"I was afraid you'd say that," Dean chuckled over his shoulder.

"Why?"

"Because," Dean said, shifting the weight in his hands to unlock the armory. "I half hoped I could dig the bullets out and melt the bastards back down again."

"I wouldn't if I were you." Truck looked at the mirror surface shining back at him. "I don't know the rules to this shindig, but I've got a feeling if you dug the silver out, the fuzzy fuckers would spring back to life."

"Eh." Dean shrugged and frowned. "Maybe I'd leave a sliver here and there. Just to keep them down."

Truck had never made ammo before, and as Dean hit his groove Truck got the distinct impression that his hovering around was more or less putting him square in the way. So, he made his way back into the dorm building to see how Violet was faring. It'd feel good to let her in on the good news about the change in their ammo situation.

The lamp on the bedside table was off, but a sliver of light from the adjoining bathroom cut through the darkness like a razor. The door was more than a little ajar, and plumes of steam made the air damp and heavy.

Truck was hard so fast he almost busted a seam in his trousers.

Violet's slender frame was just visible through the fogged glass of the shower, and she hummed lightly as she lathered herself down. After the night they had shared, the open door stood as a brazen invitation, and Truck stripped naked and geared up to RSVP.

FOURTEEN

Violet couldn't remember the last time she'd had an actual shower. They were top-tier coveted truckstop luxuries. Made for dreaming about, not actually enjoying.

The Pack wasn't exactly renowned for its hygiene. If anything, they gloried in the greasy stink that clung to their shit-stained bodies. Bathing was for the weak, and those brutes were gonna be goddamned if they let themselves seem the least bit feeble.

Truth be told, they were probably gonna be goddamned anyway.

With soap and water in short supply, when Violet did get to wash, it was a race against time to get dressed again before any of those pervy dickheads got eyes on her.

From the second her boobs started coming in, she'd been on her guard. In a world built entirely of hard roads, that was the roughest one for a girl coming into herself surrounded by unscrupulous men.

The more her woman's body crept up on her like an unwelcome thief in the night, the more Violet realized that her already shitty life was capable of getting far, far worse.

So, a private shower in a secure bunker was manna from heaven. Water had to be a precious resource, but fuck it. This might be a once in a lifetime opportunity, so she cranked the heat as high as it would go and took her damn sweet time. If there was hell to pay, she'd pick up the check later.

Then the shower door opened.

An icicle of blind panic jabbed into her ribs, and she whipped around ready to descend into the feral chaos she had so strictly forbidden herself. She lashed out with her hand, ready to smack the intruder into the middle of next year.

"Woah," Truck cried, leaning back just in time to avoid getting his cheek slashed by her fingernails. "Hey, sorry! Shit, I shouldn't have—"

"Oh," Violet exclaimed, flattening her back against the wall and covering her mouth with her hands. "No, it's—"

"I should go." He was already stepping out of the shower, but Violet caught him by the wrist. The whizzing shock of adrenaline still percolated in her blood, but a new instinct sent it rushing straight south.

"It's okay," she said, a coy smile painting her dripping lips. "It was a reflex."

"I should have known better." Truck stood shamefaced at his intrusion, and Violet could see he was still set on making an exit. But now that Violet could see his body again, there was no way she was letting him slip through her soapy fingers.

"Get in here." She gave his arm a light tug, her grin spreading into something far naughtier. "We should get you clean."

"Funny," Truck smirked back, stepping in and closing the shower door behind him, "I was planning on getting dirty."

Water cascaded over his shoulders as he towered over her, speckling her face in his shadow. Truck planted his hands on either side of Violet's head and drew so close she thought her heart would pop.

The water was scalding, but it was the heat coming off his

body that made her skin blister. She'd been so close to letting herself boil over into madness, and the raging quake of the animal inside made every inch of her feel fiendishly *alive.*

Driving her hands up along the craggy perfection of his chest, she wrapped her arms around his neck and pulled herself up to find his mouth. Her sudsy back squeaked across the wall as her feet left the floor, toes already curling from the taste of his mouth.

Truck's lips told her that he was every bit as famished as she was. They'd spent the entire night glutting themselves with each other, but her need for him was unquenchable.

"God, Violet," he groaned as he tore his mouth away to kiss the soft patch of skin below her ear. "You're irresistible." As he said it, his hands slipped down her sides, tickling at her ribs, then sweeping back to cup her ass.

Her legs leaped up to wrap around his hips and her whole body shivered as his cock slid against her. The water made his shoulders slick, so she held even tighter. Wriggling to align herself, she braced to take the heady weight of him into her body again.

"Hang on," he whispered, loosening his hold on her rear and drawing his hips away. "There's something I want to do." With a light pat on the thigh, he encouraged her to let her legs down, and as she did, he stooped so that her feet could find the shower pan.

As his mouth savaged a path down along her neck, Violet tangled her fingers in his soaking, coal dark hair. Her nipples tightened so much they stung in readiness for his mouth. But Truck left them aching, kissing his way down the center of her chest, the fringe of his mustache awakening the skin between her breasts.

Only when he reached her navel did his destination become clear, and the anxious electricity of it sent off a spray of sparks along her skin. If they hadn't been in the shower, Violet would have combusted on the spot.

Truck hung in place, probing her navel with his tongue as a tantalizing hint of what lay in store. She squirmed against the wall, impatient and bashful all at once. The path Truck carved was one she had never been down before, but she knew that if any man would patiently show her the way, it was the one kissing his way along the lowest part of her belly.

When he was fully on his knees, Truck's hands found her ass again, and laying her legs over his shoulders was the simplest, most natural thing. His breath came husky and damp, drenching her thighs with more than just water.

And then he found her.

The first furtive slash of his tongue cracked through her like a thunderbolt, and Violet arched back against the wall and her jaw locked open. Try as she might, she couldn't manage to breathe.

He licked her again, with more purpose this time, and she knotted her fingers in his hair and started to shake. Just when she thought she might die, the son of a bitch did it again.

"Fuck," she screamed, and suddenly he was everywhere at once.

Truck leaned in, and Violet fastened her ankles behind his back, slamming her knees towards each other. Now that she knew this sensation was possible, she was never going to let him get away. Her back squelched up the shower wall as Truck's furious mouth ravaged her pulsing button. Feather light flicks of the tip gave way to heavy, passionate swipes along his whole tongue.

A bomb went off in Violet's skull, scattering her thoughts like shrapnel. Every time she tried to piece something together, Truck's mouth came along to ignite another blast.

Only when her head bumped the ceiling did she realize Truck had dug into her so hard he was on his feet again. She was doubled over his head, hips rocked forward to offer every bit of herself. Racking, sobbing breaths spilled past her lips and along his back to whistle down the drain.

From the first touch she'd been in the throes of one long, rolling orgasm, and the deeper she fell into the frantic pit, the more she needed.

"Please," was the only word her lips were able to form. Just a litany of desperate, savage *please*s as she melted further and further from herself. The coil in her spine tightened to the breaking point, and she faced something her life could never have prepared her for.

The point of his tongue found her again with the devilish pressure of fast, livid swipes. She'd reached the brink, and the inevitable fall yawned before her with terrifying power. Then he slipped a finger inside her, and the world stopped spinning. The room fell in on itself and Violet went blind, lost in a maze of astounding pleasure.

When she could see again, the water was off. She was on the floor of the shower, cradled in Truck's embrace. Her legs still trembled across his, jolting now and then with a sharp spasm to remind her of the pandemonium she'd weathered. His chin rested on the top of her head, and she rubbed her cheek against his chest.

"That was..." she began to say, but Truck merely ducked a finger under her chin and tipped her head back. He kissed her with such tenderness she almost came again.

"Nobody's ever done that for me before," she said softly as they settled back into each other.

"Never?"

"The Pack's not exactly a generous, loving place."

A deep breath rattled between his ribs. Neither moved. Their bodies still fit together as perfectly as before, but the air around them shifted. Danger crept in to join them, but Violet couldn't pinpoint how.

"You said one of them tried to claim you." The way Truck

said it loitered somewhere between a statement and a question, and an ugly chill tightened Violet's chest.

"The Chamberlain, yes."

"What gave him the right?"

Violet froze. To answer that would mean revealing so many things she desperately wanted to keep hidden—especially from Truck. A deluge of guilt spilled over her, and shame crowded up in her throat.

How could I let myself get so close to him? How could I ruin his life like this?

She shrank in his lap until she felt like she might slip down the drain. Maybe it would be better for them both if she did.

"Are you crying?" Truck asked, and she realized that she was.

"I'm sorry," she whimpered, shifting away from him and pulling her knees up to her chin. "I'm so, so sorry."

"It's alright," Truck said, reaching out to place a hand on her ankle. "What did I tell you about apologizing? You don't have to do that anymore."

Violet looked into his face, more afraid than she had ever been — even more than when she was fleeing from The Pack alone and hopeless.

"I don't mean about the crying," she croaked through her strangling throat.

"Neither do I." Truck's candor caught her right in the gut. "You don't have to tell me anything you don't want to." He leaned over and kissed the top of her knee, then got to his feet and offered her his hand. "We should get dressed. Dean and I got some things started this morning."

They were still wrapped in towels when there was a knock at the door.

"I hate to break up the party." She could hear Dean's sly smile in his voice. "But you should get out here. There's some shit you need to hear."

FIFTEEN

"Check it out," Dean said as the three of them stepped back into his armory. The place smelled of gun oil, with the added edge of flame and raw powder. When Violet saw the silver on Dean's workstation, her heart leapt. She almost snatched one of the bullets to turn it over in her hands, but didn't dare.

Just touching it seemed forbidden.

Instead, Violet stood staring, salvation glittering on the shiny hollow points.

"Huh." Reaching past her, Dean cranked up the volume on his CB, with his brows bunched up. Clearly he was expecting something, but all he got was the staticky hum of an empty channel.

"I don't get it." Truck arched an eyebrow at his friend. "What are we listening for?"

"Goddamnit," Dean hissed, giving the table a thump with his fist so that the whole apparatus rattled. "I just intercepted some chatter, and I'd swear on a stack of holy fucking bibles it was your guys."

"Our guys?" Violet narrowed her eyes. Her gut rumbled. None of this seemed right. "What do you mean?"

"It was a bunch of voices talking about trying to take

down a green cab from a rig." Dean jabbed his finger towards the slumbering beast out in the yard. "Sound familiar to you two?"

Truck's whole body went taut, and he chewed his lower lip as he stared into the middle distance. "What else were they saying?" The gears were turning so fast Violet could almost see them beating in his temples. His laser focus only sharpened the uneasiness in her stomach.

"Battle plans, maybe? Here." Dean grabbed a scrap of paper with some chicken scratch on it and jammed it into Truck's hand. "I managed to get this down. It ought to mean something to you." He tapped it twice, and a confident grin cut across Truck's face.

"Gotcha, motherfuckers." The two men shared a conspiratorial, almost gleeful laugh.

"What is it?" Violet asked, hating being left out.

"Reef Ridge," Truck replied, snapping the paper down on the workbench.

"Damn straight." Dean clucked, the ruthless side of his nature itching to the surface. "Said it's their rendezvous point. They're circling up there before they launch a two pronged assault. But if we beat them to the punch..."

"They'll all be in one place," Truck finished for him, and Dean nodded.

"Bullseye."

"Where's Reef Ridge?" At her question, Dean broke out in a wicked, victorious smile.

"Less than ten miles, north-northwest," he gleamed.

"Let's move." Truck put the period on the whole confab, and the two men bolted from the table and flung themselves into gearing up. Violet stood numbly for a moment, looking between the shells, the radio, and the greasy bit of paper.

This is all wrong.

"How many rounds did you manage to get together?"

Truck called as he stuffed a satchel with grenades and mortar rounds.

"Five, six dozen," Dean answered. "And about twenty five straight up bullets for a long range rifle. It ain't much, but if we're smart about it—" He stole a glance over to where Truck was building his murderous Santa sack. "Explosives aren't silver, man. Those won't do any good."

"Their bikes aren't Werewolves," Truck shot back. "We can cripple those easy, then pick the bastards off."

"Wait," Violet said, trying to get her bearings as the two men raced around. "Something's not right."

"What do you mean?" Truck's breath was up, and she could see the blaze of battle in his eyes. Moving close, she put a hand on his arm and tried to talk to the man behind the testosterone rush.

"I don't know what it is, but this feels wrong. Like it's a trap or something. Rushing out there is a bad idea."

"Better than waiting here," Dean chimed in, strapping into a Kevlar vest. "Trap or no trap, if we can hit them head on with the firepower we've got, we can at least punch a hole in them."

"Maybe," Violet said, her stomach squirmier than a bait shop. "But, Truck?" She caught his eyes again. "It's a miracle your rig survived against them this long. If you start throwing grenades, she'll never last."

"Oh, we're not taking Layla." Dean's laugh cut through the powder flooded air. "Check this out." He darted through the door, and Violet and Truck trotted after him, her skin chilled even under the scorching midday sun.

Dean started heaving old tires and bits of junk off a large, tarp covered mountain. Tugging at ropes and edges, he sent bungee straps sailing off into the breeze in his excitement. When enough were free, he whipped around to face Truck and Violet with an almost deranged grin.

"You wanna see some wild shit?" Not waiting for a reply,

he whipped off the final oil stained tarp to reveal a terrifying, steel plated vehicle. Somewhere between an armadillo and a scorpion, it hugged low to the ground glaring ferociously back at them.

There were slits for visibility, but that was all the purchase it offered to the outside world. Even the wheel beds were covered. Each one had a hole large enough for a long, screw shaped spike to jut out. The whole thing was studded with steel skewers, and a covered turret at the top boasted an array of nasty looking muzzles.

"Are you for real?" Truck said, awe struck as a seven year old boy. Now that this thing was out in the open, there was no way Violet was going to be able to keep them from rushing off to war.

"Built on a military chassis and all but unflippable," Dean boasted. "The underside is all steel plated, so there's no going under to fuck up all the fiddly bits."

"What do you call this thing?" Truck asked, testing one of the points with the flat of his palm.

"The Pequod."

Truck let out a whoop of laughter, but Violet only wilted further. Dean knocked one of the hatches open, and the two men crowed merrily as they stuffed the death machine to the brim with weapons.

It was a boys-will-be-boys free for all. Violet trailed along behind them, trying like hell to figure out how to reason her way through their manic, schoolyard zeal.

"Truck," she said, cornering him in the armory as he rummaged through a bin of explosives. "Please don't do this. I don't like it."

"Violet..." He reached out and placed a palm on her cheek. "I understand you're worried. But it's going to come to a fight one way or the other. Why not take the fight to them and do as much damage as we can?"

"I guess." She shrugged, "But -" Truck took her wrist and planted a kiss in the center of her palm.

"It's going to be alright. I can feel it."

"If you say so," she said, refusing to give in to the sinking feeling brimming in her chest. "But I'm coming with you."

That sobered Truck right the hell up, and he set his armload back down and held Violet's shoulders to face her directly.

"I can't let you do that."

"Why," she countered. "Because it's not safe? If that's why, then you shouldn't go running off into this either."

"It's not that. It's just..." He looked over her shoulder, and Violet glanced back to catch Dean pretending not to watch. "We need you here." It was the last thing she expected him to say, and she snapped her attention back to him.

"You're not going to leave me alone, are you?" Just thinking it sent her anxiety bubbling over into actual fear.

"It would be too risky to take you out where they could get you again. Besides, we'll need somebody here manning the radio and relaying to us if something comes up. Not only that," a rakish smile tugged at the corner of his mouth, "who's going to let us back in?"

Finally, an actual reason. The stronghold had been built to keep folks out, and that meant someone needed to be on the inside to make sure things stayed locked up tight.

Logical? Sure.

But logic wasn't worth a damn in a world of Werewolves and silver bullets. Violet caught Truck's hand between hers, tangling her fingers between his and dropping her voice.

"Truck, please?" Pouring every ounce of her latent vulnerability into her eyes, she implored him not to do this. His lip twitched, and for a second she could tell she was getting through to him. The Truck who cared for her was starting to seep back to the surface.

Then an impossible roar gutted the sky, rattling the stronghold down to its foundation. Dean had fired up the Pequod, and Truck's head snapped around, eyes prying at the armory door.

There was no keeping him.

She was so close, and now she'd lost her hopes with the single turn of a key. Dean Harris knew what he was doing, alright. There was no way Truck would be able to resist the siren song of a murder wagon drag race.

When Truck looked at her again, the deal was done. He was going, and that was that.

"Fine," she said at last, lifting his hand to dust his knuckles with her lips. "But promise to come back in one piece." Truck took her in his arms, leaning over her to brush his mouth over hers.

"Violet, I promise." He kissed her, and the two of them walked out to see the land-bound leviathan first hand. Afraid as she was, Violet had to admire the raw power of the rumbling monstrosity.

It was a tank. More than a tank, it was a solid steel death machine. She just hoped it was built to keep death on the *outside*.

Now that she and Truck had fully found each other, the idea of losing him made her want to rip herself to shreds. They'd shared so much more than just their bodies, reshaping anything she'd ever dreamed her life could be. Surely he had to feel that too?

He does. I know he does.

But there was no stopping this. All she could do was trust that he knew what he was doing.

Up to this point, Violet had learned firsthand that Truck never boasted of anything he couldn't back up. Now it was time to cross all her fingers and toes and hope that his luck held out.

After she locked the gate behind them, Violet looked up

the precarious ladder up to the water tower. Its dizzying angle wasn't exactly inviting, but in the opposite corner was a broad set of welded steps that snaked up to the catwalk.

Scaling those, she wound around to the water tower and watched the homemade tank furrowing up the desert floor. It grew smaller and smaller as the cloud of dust it kicked up grew, and a dreadful nagging feeling refused to surrender its falcon grip on her heart.

Life in the desert hadn't given her much time to read up on the classics, but there was one thing she knew for certain.

The Pequod sank.

SIXTEEN

"This thing is incredible," Truck said, standing in the turret, gawking at the array of weapons. There was enough firepower in six square feet to make General Patton's dick hard from beyond the grave.

"Yeah, man." Dean chuckled from behind the wheel. "I've been Frankensteining this bitch together for years. Every once in a while something hits me, and I break out the welding gear and get to work."

"It's one hell of a machine." Truck scrunched back down to shove shells full of silver shot into Pepper. Dean craned his neck to see what Truck was up to and gave him a nod.

"If I was you I'd focus on jamming some of those .45s into the Aero I've got mounted up in the fire station there. The shotgun is a good second string, but my hope is we'll use that to clean up after we've scorched the earth."

"I like the way you think." Rummaging around in his pack, Truck came up with a leather pouch filled with his buddy's handiwork. As he spilled out the pinkie-sized rounds into his waiting hand, he was struck by how they glistened, even in the low light stealing in through the slits in the barnyard bruiser.

Goddamn, Truck thought, slotting bullet after bullet into

the magazine. *We've actually got this. It's going to be lights-out for those filthy dickheads.*

"You're gonna want to strap in," Dean called as the Pequod picked up speed. "We're gonna hit Reef Ridge in less than a minute."

"Roger." Truck took in the gunner's station and got to work.

Dean had repurposed an old EMT spine board, bolted to a pivot in the floor. It hung with more straps than a stepdad's pickup bed, and Truck cinched himself in place. With one foot on the pivot and the other on the floorboard, he could rotate himself from one gunstock to the next with startling ease.

"This must be what God feels like," he muttered, and Dean clucked out a small laugh.

"You said it. Now what say we give these sons of bitches a little bit of that old time religion?"

"Gun it," Truck ordered.

Determined to make a hero's entrance, Dean plowed his way up a rugged jut of caliche that gave the ridge its name, and the cast iron battleship grabbed air as they surged into the blast zone. It clapped to the soil again with an ear shattering crunch that was sure to leave Mother Earth with a black eye to explain to the neighbors.

In any other universe, a stunt like that would have busted all four tires on the three ton scrap heap, but Dean's creation kept right on rolling, kicking up a bushel of stinging gravel in its wake. They slued into the open, sawing their way through the dirt as they fishtailed a hole in the mesquite bushes.

"I got eyes on a bike," Dean shouted.

"Where?"

"Two o'clock. That one of your boys?"

Truck squinted through the viewing slit, grinding his foot onto the floor to spin his captain's chair to get a better angle. Sure as shit, a fierce, rusted jalopy was dead in his sights, and sitting astride it was a mangy manbeast with its tongue hanging loose out of its gaping maw.

"Damn straight," Truck yelled back. He knew who it was without having to be told. Even knowing these bastards had perpetual bounce back potential, it ruffled him to see the bastard he'd pancaked the day before back in action. "That one's called Scum."

"It suits him," Dean laughed. "Fire at will."

"You don't have to tell me twice." Yanking back on the bolt to chamber one of those sterling widowmakers, Truck braced the barrel, sited, and held his breath to keep his aim true. The shitty news was, he could be as still as a dead man and wouldn't have a chance in hell of hitting the broad side of a barn.

The Pequod was many things, but a smooth ride wasn't on the list. Especially as it chomped across the desert floor.

"How close can you get me?" Truck hissed. "Can't get a steady shot at this distance while we're moving."

"Sorry about that." Dean cringed up at him. "This was built to be a one man operation. Charge in, park, and open shop."

"I hear you," Truck said, and at that moment Scum got wind of them and kicked his starter pedal to peel off. "We might just get our chance. That dumb son of a bitch is gonna lead us right into the honeypot. Stay on his tail."

"Way ahead of you." Dean cut the wheel like it owed him money, and despite being bound tighter than a goddamn mummy, Truck almost pitched clean out of the turret. The low center of gravity kept the tank from flipping over, but a hanger like that all but lifted the tires up.

Scum was at high noon in Truck's vision, and Dean bore down on him with intent to run the bastard over for the second time. They closed ground fast, and Truck did what he could to draw a bead right between Scum's pointy ears.

Before he could squeeze the trigger, Scum let out a

terrible howl and kicked up into a wheelie. It must have been some kind of signal because a half dozen Werewolves stormed out of the scrub to join the fun. Guns drawn, they sent round after round pinging off old ironsides until sparks flew.

"Jesus H. Shit," Truck hollered as still more monsters swarmed around them. "They're everywhere!"

"Take it easy," Dean said. "This is what the Pequod was built for. Nothing bigger than a .22 is gonna get through the viewing slits, and even that would take dead aim on level ground."

"If you say so."

Truck wasn't entirely convinced, but what was he gonna do? In less than fifteen seconds they were in it up to the ankles. All they could do now was bring the rumpus.

Swinging himself behind the butt of a scattergun, Truck looked for a spot to punch a hole in their offensive line. Trouble was, it was like the bastards knew what he was about, and any time he sighted on a clutch of them, they fanned out again.

The whole party thundered forward in a cyclone of rusted metal and dirt, ducking and weaving in a dreadful ballet of imminent carnage.

"Truck?" The radio fizzed to life, and Violet's voice ran up Truck's spine like a rat.

"He's a little tied up at the moment," Dean answered into the receiver. "What's up?"

"It's a trap," she cried.

"We figured that one out," Dean said with cool control.

"Come back," she pleaded. "Fast as you can—they're going to do something big." If Truck had been on his own, he might have given in to her, but the man at the helm had other ideas.

"Negative," Dean replied. "Dean Harris never backs down from a fight."

Truck knew it was true, but what he might have once considered his friend's courage was starting to look an awful lot like hubris. Sweat poured down Dean's neck, and his eyes had the glassy, crazed look of a combat vet who's seen far too much. Which, Truck realized, is exactly who he was locked in this wrought iron coffin with.

"Maybe she's right."

That's what Truck was going to say. But then The Pequod crested a berm, and he choked on the first syllable.

No sooner had they touched down than they were caught across the prow by a hefty run of chain strung between two oil drums. The damn things must have been filled with concrete because they held fast, pulling the death machine to a stop so short it was God's own miracle they didn't flip over.

"Fuck," Truck snorted, the straps digging into him with the force of the strike. His loose arms flailed forward to bust his knuckles on the inside of the turret. Dean suffered a similar fate, his knees banging the underside of the dash hard enough to shatter his kneecaps.

"Oh, goddamnit!" Dean wheezed and doubled over, his hands abandoning the wheel to clamp over his pulverized knees. What momentum the Pequod still had sent it careening sideways, juddering over rocks and kicking up a choking cloud of dirt.

They scrunched to a stop, the pitched angle of their vehicle removing any doubt that they'd obliterated a couple of tires. Shit, they'd probably snapped an axel pulling that stunt.

To make matters worse, the engine banged and shuddered from the damage the chain had done. Riding the Pequod further into combat was out of the question. At this point, they'd be lucky if they could limp the damn thing home.

"How you doing down there, champ?" Truck called.

"I'll live," Dean answered through gritted teeth.

"If we get out of this." Truck more than half meant it, and Dean coughed out a thin laugh.

"This is what the old girl was designed for," he said. "Like I said, park and spit lead. Or, in this case, silver." Dean cut his eyes up to Truck, every inch the boyhood friend who knew just what a dare meant. "Ball's in your court, Truck! This is your turkey shoot now."

That was all the reminder Truck needed, and he returned to the task at hand.

Now that the rig wasn't leaping all over the place, he was able to draw a cleaner bead on things. Hugging up to the Aero, he scanned the rabble to pick a brute to dethrone. Scum was nowhere to be seen, nor was The Chamberlain. After that prick had snatched up Violet, Truck had a bone to pick with that particular hound.

Deciding to sow a little random chaos, Truck picked some unlucky beast and lined up the crosshairs right between its livid yellow eyes. He cracked off a shot, and the thing pitched backwards off his bike with a yelp.

His compatriots snarled and gunned their engines, riding up a tempest as they waited for the poor fucker to right himself. But when that didn't happen, they slowed their circles, ultimately stopping in stunned realization.

This tank was packing silver.

That razor thin moment of stillness was the engraved invitation Truck was waiting for.

He aimed again, readying to destroy as many as he could while they were frozen with shock. Another bullet cleaned out another Wolf, and Truck lined up for a third.

"That's the goddamn spirit," Dean cheered him on. "Punch 'em full of holes!"

A bellow splintered the desert air, swiftly followed by the ungodly shriek of an engine. Whipping himself around on the pivot, Truck squinted through a slit to size up the hell getting ready to rain down.

It was The Duke.

Because of fucking course it was.

His eyes blazed red, and his mouth yawned wide in a malevolent snarl. The bike between his legs was like something out of legend. Bigger than goddamn Clydesdale, and covered in jagged spikes from handlebars to taillight. A sidecar added to the bulk, but instead of a passenger, something far more lethal was headed their way.

It was another oil drum, and while Truck couldn't swear to the contents, a flaming rag flapping at the top gave him a hint. The leader of The Pack was bearing down on them with a 50-gallon Molotov bomb. Something that size could burn for days, charring Truck and Dean blacker than your mother-in-law's Christmas turkey.

"I've got bad news, Dean," Truck muttered.

"I got eyes on him." Dean's voice was measured and grim. Then he shrugged it off and sat up so brightly it made the hairs on Truck's arms stand on end. "You know what? Fuck it." Dean kicked his seatbelts loose and heaved himself up in his chair with an agonized groan.

"The fuck are you doing, man?"

"Buying you some time," Dean answered, dragging himself towards the hatch. He twisted the crank that opened the trap door, and Truck's brain exploded.

"Like hell you are," he growled, tugging at straps in a desperate bid to set himself free.

"Don't worry, Tucker." The sound of his real name pulled Truck up short, and he met his friend's pale blue eyes. Far from madness, they were startlingly calm. "I'll be sure and tell Jenn you say hi." With that, he kicked the portal open, drew his pistol, and let loose with a war cry.

Dean vanished into the white hot afternoon, and Truck snapped his gaze back to the viewing slit in his turret.

The Duke was right on top of them, his great paw bucking against the lip of the barrel to work it free. His lupine face slackened in amazement as Dean "Fox" Harris's wiry frame sprang through the air. He connected with the flaming drum, toppling it, The Duke, and the whole caboodle into an inferno Satan himself would be proud of.

It was the ultimate act of pure selflessness, the cleansing fire blasting away any blemishes on Dean's life. Truck's heart balled up so tight it got a charley horse. Estranged though they might have been, Dean and Truck were brothers. Tripping head first into a chasm of heartbreak would have been perilously easy - there just wasn't time for it.

Dean had leaped into the flaming jaws of death with open arms, and there was no way in bitter hell Truck was going to let it be for nothing.

"Now or never," Truck hissed to himself, biting through the waterboard gag of grief. Snatching up stocks, he started taking potshots at anything with teeth. His first one landed true, sending a furry shitheel sprawling backwards out of the saddle. The bike wobbled forward and slammed into the front quarter of the Pequod, ringing the whole interior with the sound of impact.

Truck continued cranking the trigger, but thanks to the tears stinging his eyes, more than half the shots went wild. Wasting silver was a losing proposition, so he let his hand fall.

Good news was the Pequod had avoided a direct hit from the makeshift bomb. Bad news was the blaze was close enough that things were heating up fast. Truck could have fried a whole dozen eggs on the windward side.

Not only that, Dean hadn't exactly taken the time to shut the portal behind him, which left Truck strapped to a board while the whole world looked in at his sitting duck ass.

All this added up to one thing.

Truck needed to abandon ship before shit outside settled down enough for them to think of coming into the sardine can to get him.

An automatic rifle jutted to one side, and while it wasn't silver loaded, it would offer cover. Truck squeezed the trigger with one hand and ripped at his straps with the other. He was free just as the soles of his shoes threatened to melt to the pivot platform.

Drenched in sweat, he crouched to snatch Pepper up from the floorboard. She was blisteringly hot to the touch, but she was also brim full of silver shot. There was no question of leaving her behind. He was just gonna have to grin and bear it.

After being inside that rolling bunker, the full desert sun damn near blinded Truck.

Scrunching his eyes to slits, he cast his gaze down long enough to see the sputtering heap of what used to be Dean Harris. The sight choked him, and his head spun.

The guy was worth gallons of tears, but Truck knew better than to stand around weeping over spilt blood. Pulling that shit would just mean his friend died in vain, and he'd be goddamned if he let a man like Dean Harris waste himself.

If anything, Dean would have busted Truck's ass for getting all emotional when it was time to get shit done – and there was a whole heaping mountain of shit that needed doing.

There wasn't a whiff of burnt dog on the breeze, and worse yet, no trace of The Duke in the billowing flames. The fucker had managed to escape going up in smoke.

Which meant it was time to get moving.

Doubling down, Truck chugged across the top of the Pequod towards the front and looked down. A riderless bike lay on its side, engine still rumbling. Truck wasn't much of a motorcycle rider, but he knew better than to count a gift horse's teeth.

In a flash, he was down in the dirt, working like hell to yank the thing upright.

A bloodthirsty growl put Truck on the offensive, and he

lifted Pepper just in time to pump one of the devils full of pellets. The Wolf jerked out of its seat, and as the bike swerved along riderless, Truck took opportunity by the tits. He grabbed the handles as it shuddered past, kicked himself over the top, and wrenched the throttle.

In the twinkling of a thigh, Truck was in the saddle, ripping across the prairie. He knew the general direction they had come from, but if he got some open horizon, he was sure the compound would be pretty easy to spot.

Leaning low over the spine of his stolen chopper, he opened her all the way up. If the big idea was to lure Truck and Dean into a trap, then it was a fair bet some stragglers hung back to see if they could crack the egg and steal Violet. The thought alone was enough to make Truck rise out of the seat in an effort to make the hellbeast between his legs go even faster.

The image of Violet in peril pinched him more than he could have ever imagined, and he had to admit that maybe it was more than just a protective streak spurring him on.

His whole life, Truck had scrupulously avoided the big 'L,' and now he may have tripped backwards and tugged the goddamn word into his rig.

It was something he'd have to unpack when he had the breathing room because regardless of whether members of The Pack had hung back to try and nab his girl, a glimpse in the rear view mirror told Truck there was still plenty of fight riding up behind him.

SEVENTEEN

Even with the sun boiling down out of the desert sky, Violet shivered. Tired of watching the horizon in vain, she hugged herself and went down to the armory. Not that it gave her any real reprieve. She just wound up pacing the floor in a cold sweat.

The light static on the radio taunted her so bad it was all she could do not to yank the thing down and batter it to pieces with a hammer.

Of course it was a trap.

The instant she'd closed the doors behind Truck and Dean, she could feel it. The radio remained silent, only proving the communication as a ruse. She squeezed her eyes shut, kicking herself for not doing more to stop the guys before they rode out on their suicide mission.

All she could do was hope that Dean had done Yeoman's work cranking out enough silver bullets to do some real damage. Because leaving the job half done would only be poking the bear with a stick of dynamite.

In the end, there was only one of those monsters she really needed to see dead. Maybe two, but The Duke's death was the one her entire future depended on. If he was still walking the earth in three days' time, then Violet might as well give Truck a pat on the butt and ride off with The Pack for good.

"Violet..." A harsh voice taunted her from the radio, sending goosebumps racing over her skin. "We know you're in there..."

The singsong mock left no doubt who was on the other end of the line—

The Chamberlain.

His lascivious, sneering tone shot through her veins in an icy shudder. She wanted to grab the receiver and tell him all the places he could stick it, but her voice abandoned her.

"The Duke blew up that junk heap rig your heroes came to chase us with. How about you be a good girl? Open the door and let us in."

What?

It had to be a bluff. There's no way The Pack could have destroyed that welded steel monstrosity Dean Harrison had breathed life into... right?

"Nobody's coming to rescue you, Vee." The dirtbag was slobbering so hard the radio was dripping. "Little pig, little pig, let me in..."

He was lying. He had to be.

Even if wasn't, Violet's stomach shrank in on itself so much she almost doubled over onto the floor.

She had to find out for herself. Staggering across the armory on unsteady legs, Violet burst through the door and out into the dusty yard.

Even above the top of the massive walls, she could see a blotch of black smoke choking the sky. Her heart slammed into her throat, and she raced to the base of a ladder, jagging up the side of the front tower. It may have spooked her earlier, but the time for petty fear was over.

Hand over sweaty hand she hurled herself up, her feet barely touching the rungs as she dragged herself to the catwalk. The spindly ladder shook and bowed under her, but she gritted her teeth and kept climbing. If the whole thing broke free and sent her crashing to the hard desert floor, so fucking be it.

Because on the off chance that The Chamberlain was telling the truth, a world without Truck Laine wasn't a world she wanted to live in.

By the time she reached the top, her pulse battered the inside of her ribs. There was something out there alright, but no matter how she stared and shielded her eyes, they refused to focus.

Violet couldn't let herself believe what she was seeing. A thick glut of ugly smoke bloomed from behind some crags in the distance, and from hard experience, she knew the source was a bonfire of gasoline and oil. She'd seen more vehicle fires than hot breakfasts, and her heart dropped through the soles of her ratty shoes, all the way down to the dust eighteen feet below.

"Hey, princess," a voice called up to her, and when Violet dropped her gaze, her whole body quaked in terror. Just below her on the outside of the enclosure stood The Chamberlain, his mouth carved into an evil, victorious grin. "I was wondering if you were going to answer."

He held up a CB radio receiver, winked at her, and let it drop into the sidecar of his chopper. All she wanted to do was spit down into his face, but she was so high up he'd be able to get out of the way before it even got close. Or worse, he might just open his mouth and try to catch it.

"I've missed you," he said, running the flat of his hand along the steel wall and drumming his fingers at her. "How about you be a good girl and open the doors for us? I promise I'll be gentle... the first time."

"Liar," his companion chortled, and Violet flicked her attention over to the greasy, fat figure of Mordred. That motherfucker had been trying to get his sausage link fingers on her every bit as eagerly as The Chamberlain, and Violet paled at the thought of either of them getting in.

"The first time is special, ain't it, princess?" The Chamberlain cooed. "Once you're bound to me, the real party can start. Who knows?" He cut a lewd look to his riding companion. "Maybe after a while, I'd feel generous enough to share."

They laughed amongst themselves, and Violet all but fainted on the spot. If she did, she'd have to make sure she tipped backwards into the enclosure. No sense in giving those bastards an easy shot at a free meal.

Her vision greyed out, and just before it abandoned her altogether, a sound ripped her back to herself. It was one she knew to depths of her soul – a bike blazing along at top speed. Others joined in the chorus, but one engine whined higher than all the rest.

"You've got to be fucking kidding me," The Chamberlain muttered, and despite how far she was above him, Violet could hear the utter disbelief in his voice. A flash of hope sparked in her chest, and she lifted her chin to squint into an approaching dust cloud. When she did, she damn near grew wings and flew off.

It's Truck.

Even at that distance, there was no doubt in her mind. She'd admired each facet of his body, and now that she'd come to learn them firsthand, she would have known him anywhere.

He had a narrow lead, but at least it was a lead. Truck was bent low over the prow of a desert bike, making the most of it.

Fanned out behind him was the full power of The Pack, churning up a massive red cloud that billowed behind them. It was a terrifying scene, but Violet couldn't help smiling in spite of it all.

Because the one thing she hoped for in the whole pig fucking universe came up aces for her.

Truck was alive.

That meant there was still a chance things could sort themselves out.

Problem was – and it was a big fucking problem – The Chamberlain and Mordred were basically guarding the entrance. Even if Violet managed to open the doors in time for Truck to slip through, it was almost certain that they'd have some bitter goddamn company to show for it.

"Fuck it." It was a risk worth taking. Whatever Truck had been through out there, Violet would rather burn in hell than leave that man to the ruthless will of The Pack.

Gripping the top of the ladder, she rode it like a fireman's pole all the way back down. Her feet slammed against the hard ground, sending a splintering ache up each shin.

She didn't have time to indulge the pain. There was bigger shit to be done.

Falling into a dead sprint, Violet dove back into the armory and grabbed the first weapon that came to hand. It was a double bladed axe with a head so heavy it stretched her shoulder as she lugged it back to the doors.

There was no telling what she'd actually be able to do with the damn thing, but she'd burn that bridge when she came to it.

EIGHTEEN

Truck spotted the most dazzling beacon in the history of mankind – Violet at the top of the watchtower, shining brighter than the sun. It was all he needed to double down and make that throttle his bitch.

The engine ran so high it threatened to burn holes through his jeans, but Truck couldn't manage to give a shit. Let 'em burn. It's not like he needed them when Violet was around anyway. Hell, if they made it through this, he might never wear pants again.

Thinking like that was putting the cart before the horsepower.

First, he needed to get the upper hand, and he had no doubt that that petite girl with the heart of a lion was gonna do what she could to give it to him.

Later he'd make it a point to give it back to her – as hard and as long as he could manage.

When Violet's silhouette vanished from the upper ledge, Truck knew in his bones he could count on those massive doors to swing open any time. The trick was not letting the whole band of marauders in behind him. But if anybody could manage it, Violet could.

No sooner had he thought it than Truck got a gander at

the mini-ambush awaiting him. Two grimy shitheels caught wind of his approach and started contorting in their saddles. Human faces fell away, shoulders bulked with muscle and fur, claws sprang up where fingernails once were.

The sight went and ruined an already piss poor afternoon.

"Great," he muttered. "Just fucking great."

The Pack was hot on his heels, and Truck knew without looking that every man of them was in full Wolf mode. Their howls shredded his already frayed nerves, and now he had two more dead in front of him to deal with.

But there was one lesson the road had taught him good and well.

The only way out is through.

Whipping Pepper up from his side and laying her across the handlebars, he was determined to make the expression *dead in front of him* a literal fucking reality.

It was hard to keep the ragged chopper on a straight path with one hand, but he needed to rack the shotgun, so tough shit. He was fresh out of options. It was rough going, but he managed to chamber a round without flipping the bike, so he'd have to count that as victory number one.

Pot shots were all he was gonna get, so he had to make them count. Best to wait until he was closer before taking his chances.

The Chamberlain. In spite of all the bad luck breaking his way, a satisfied smile swiped across Truck's lips.

"Nice."

He'd have known that rangy fucker anywhere thanks to the grey and black fur shagging down his shoulders. Lousy part was the chances of hitting him were whisker slim, and Truck was in the market for a sure thing.

That meant the pot-bellied Wolf on the left drew the short straw.

Just as he readied to pull the trigger, the steel gate started to creep open. Which was a good thing because Truck wasn't itching to play Ring-Around-the-Rosie with this crew.

Both The Chamberlain and Fat Wolf looked at the opening gate in astonishment, and that was all the distraction Truck needed. Squeezing off a round, he blasted fatso straight to hell. Steaming red-black blood spattered the steel wall, scaring The Chamberlain so bad he must have shit his britches and the sidecar to boot. Cranking his hog with a yelp, The Chamberlain launched into action and fishtailed off.

Pulling his knees tight as he could to the blistering sides of his mount, Truck shot the moon and whistled into the compound. Violet yelled something as he passed, but he couldn't make out what it was.

She was having one hell of a time swinging the titanic door shut again, so Truck bagged out and tumbled in the dirt as the filched bike slammed into a mountain of used tires.

On his feet in a flash, Truck cannonballed to Violet's side, giving his all to seal The Pack on the outside of the party.

"Fuck," he grunted as a bike scraped past and snarled into the courtyard. The gate clanged shut, and he leaned against it with everything he had, turning to keep an eye on their unwelcome guest. Daring a look back at her, Truck asked, "You good to lock this thing up?"

Violet gave a tight nod, and Truck fetched a quick kiss. When he pulled back, her wide eyes sparkled with constellations shaped like hearts.

"For luck," he said, then surged away from her to meet the slavering asshole head on. Pepper lay in the dust, and Truck made a beeline straight for the only guaranteed silver shot in the whole joint.

The brute on the bike had a solid idea what was in the shotgun, and whipped in vicious circles between Truck and his trusty sidearm. There was no getting close to Pepper like this, so Truck had to change tactics.

What he needed was something to unseat the fuzzball. Get the prick on even footing. Sure, he was gearing up to ring the bell with a fucking Werewolf, but once its paws were on terra firma, Truck was sure he'd be able to manage something.

Sprinting around the perimeter, Truck scanned for anything to mete out a Grade-A clobbering. In the midst of his search, an agonizing scream from the gate had him skidding to a halt.

"Truck!"

What he saw frosted his veins.

Violet had her back to the door, her heels digging furrows in the arid ground. Her panic stricken eyes bulged wide, her whole body rigid trying to keep back a fresh intruder. But that demon was literally hell bent on making her work for it.

A thick, hairy arm jutted through the opening, clamping across her chest. Evil looking nails sank into Violet's exposed shoulder, and bright blood trickled down her upper arm.

Twenty gigatons of pure napalm exploded in Truck's skull, blowing away everything but the need to obliterate anyone or *anything* that dared to hurt her.

The world sped up and slowed down at the same time.

He chugged across the yard, teeth bared. Violet's pleading eyes were all he could see, and he sent her promise after silent promise as he thundered toward her.

Even the Wolf on the motorcycle didn't stand a chance. He whipped around to try and cut Truck off, but Truck leapt feet first through the air with a kick so ferocious it sent the monster sprawling.

Landing without missing a step, Truck galloped to Violet and crashed into the gate next to her. The power of his impact made the whole compound shake, and with a spasm and a crunch of bone, the claws released Violet. She collapsed to the ground, and Truck stepped over her defensively.

Taking the wrist of the flailing Werewolf arm in both

hands, Truck twisted and pulled as he shouldered the gate closed with all the strength he had. Whatever lupine bitch was on the losing side of things screeched and bellowed, but the steel slammed into place and Truck yanked the arm free. It landed in the dirt with a meaty thump, twitching and spurting as it tried to scratch life back into its stump.

Sliding the main bolt in place, Truck reached down for Violet and took her trembling hand.

"Can you stand?"

She nodded, staring up at him in utter amazement.

"Thank God. Hit the rest of these locks." He grabbed the severed Werewolf arm from the dust and hefted it like a club. "I'll take care of him."

The Wolf he'd kicked off its bike lay on his back gaping at Truck. The look of petrified bewilderment in his yellow eyes and slack jaw were enough to make Truck's dick weigh fifty pounds.

"Feel pretty dumb right now, don't you?" Truck said, striding towards the cowering monster. The Wolf scrambled backwards, and every time he tried to get up, Truck delivered a punishing blow with the severed arm. He beat that Werewolf like it insulted his mama, relishing each groveling whimper.

At last, Truck had whipped the beast close enough to Pepper that grabbing her up was as easy as picking a daisy. Chambering a round, he stuffed the muzzle in the Wolf's dazed, bloodied mouth.

"Please," the monster begged around the barrel. "Please."

"Please is for pussies," Truck sneered. "This one's for Dean." One flick of his finger and its head vanished into a mist of brains and hair.

Did it feel glorious to ignore the pitiful pleading?

Hundred percent.

Did it touch his sorrow over the death of his friend?

Nope. Not by a long shot.

But grief was gonna have to take a number.

Violet crouched against the gate, her hand clamped over her bleeding shoulder. The sight was enough to make Truck want to rip himself to pieces if it meant she could be whole again. But they were well past that now.

Because if all the midnight movies of his misspent childhood were true, this wasn't just some casual graze she'd gotten. That scratch might just be enough to change the course of her whole life.

And if Violet's life changed, then Truck's life went right into the bargain.

NINETEEN

"How bad is it?" Truck was at her side, the fury of moments before melted under the tender heat of his care for her. Violet trembled all over, gripping her shoulder hard.

Please no, she thought. *Not now. Not like this.*

"I'll live," she said. The blood had already stopped, and she kept her hand in place more to cover how quickly she was healing than hold her flesh together.

From the second she'd laid eyes on the man who'd come to be her savior, she'd dreaded this moment. Now there was no hiding her secret, and it was bound to change everything between them.

"Truck driver!" A ragged, resonant voice eviscerated the afternoon, sending a new wave of abject terror through Violet's bones. It was a voice she'd hoped never to hear again.

The Duke.

"Truck driver," he bellowed again. "Get out where I can see you!"

She bit her lip knowing she and Truck were now lined up for a full reckoning.

"Son of a bitch," Truck muttered under his breath. "Stay

out of sight," he told her. "I need to show these bastards I mean business." He rose to his feet and stalked over to the mutilated lump of flesh that had once been a member of The Pack.

With one swift move, Truck slung the carcass onto his shoulder and made his way to the steel steps leading to the top of the wall.

"What are you doing?" she asked. Truck cut his eyes over to her as he ascended.

"Making a point."

Unable to stop herself, Violet scrabbled to her feet. An invisible thread bound her to this man, and she mounted the steps behind him, trembling in anticipation of what she knew was waiting for them.

When they came to the catwalk along the upper perimeter, a baleful chorus of animal cries went up. Truck's steely composure never faltered, and he hoisted the ruined corpse of their comrade for all to see.

"Any of you guys want this?" he hectored them. "We don't need it stinking up the place." He hurled the body over the side, and it plummeted to the hard desert dirt, landing with a sickening crunch.

The Wolves drew back, staring at the body and choking back bile. For creatures who dealt out death so gleefully, they sure were chickenshit when one of their own got the dirty end of the stick.

"Plenty more where that came from," Truck roared. "Now get the fuck out of here before I really get angry." His wrath all but doubled him in size, and Violet tucked herself behind him as she searched down among the faces. Some were still lupine, but others had reverted to their desert-baked human forms.

"Don't make promises you're not ready to keep."

The Duke strode forward, and his subjects parted to make way for him. His long, silver hair swept around his massive shoulders in the breeze, and the unforgiving sun made his eyes shine. He may have been talking to Truck, but his gaze never left Violet. A malicious smile curled the corners of his mouth as he bored into her.

"I'm more than ready to keep that promise," Truck replied coolly. "Try me." The Duke just chuckled and shook his head as the rest of The Pack joined in the low, vicious laugh.

"You haven't told him, have you?" The wicked delight in The Duke's voice shrank Violet's stomach to a frigid pebble. She hated how much he enjoyed ruining her in the eyes of the man she'd come to depend on so dearly.

"Told me what?" Truck's voice faltered just a bit. He eyed her over his shoulder, suspicion already creeping in behind his pupils. It was enough to make Violet want to fling herself over the wall as well. As if the fall would make any difference.

"Oh, Truck driver," The Duke gloated. "Take a good look at us." He spread his arms, and his army of loathsome deviants straightened their spines. "You know what we are. And by now I imagine you've got a pretty good idea of just how long we've made this desert our kingdom. Taking what we please, when we please. Life is cheaper than scrub brush, and you've seen the proof. Now you have to ask yourself, what is it about *one silly girl* that would make us chase you like this? You'd think there were plenty of others we could ride out and snatch, wouldn't you?"

"Not like her," Truck spat back as she quaked behind him.

"That's true!" The Duke stabbed his finger up at Truck, his devilish smile deepening. "You don't know how right you are. But you're just thinking about her pretty face and those helpless, please-save-me eyes. She's delicate, isn't she? It almost makes you wonder..." He trailed off, clearly savoring in the whole thing. Truck shot another wary look over his shoulder, and the inevitable revelation twisted Violet's guts until she thought she'd die. "How is it that such a tender little lamb could survive amongst monsters like us for so long? So curious..." The Duke scrubbed his chin in a pantomime of puzzling out the mystery. It was the kind of playacting The Duke loved, and Violet was ready to plunge down just to scratch out his eyes.

"Get to the fucking point, asshole," Truck rumbled, as fed up with the whole charade as Violet was.

"The point is this." The Duke rested his foot on a nearby chopper and leaned on his thigh as he grinned up at them. "Violet there isn't just some wilting flower we kidnapped to drag around with us. Oh, no. It's better than that, truck driver. So much better—she's one of us."

Violet's throat slammed shut, and she clutched at the back of Truck's shirt to keep from dropping to her knees. Even though he didn't turn around, she could feel Truck's unease rippling through the cabled sinews of his back.

"What do you mean, one of you?" Truck asked hoarsely.

"I never introduced myself." The Duke stood to his full height, baring his tattooed, sunburnt chest with malignant pride. "I'm known as The Duke, but my name is Chance Summers. And Violet there?" He pointed to her, wickedness spilling off him in rich, stinking waves. "Well, Violet Summers is my daughter."

If Violet hadn't been holding him, Truck might have tipped forward and cratered to the ground. He gripped the railing, and Violet cringed away from him.

"*What?*" Truck barely whispered it, but the betrayal in his voice sliced her like a billion tiny razors – silver ones.

"Don't believe me?" The Duke chortled with ghastly satisfaction. "There's a full moon tomorrow night. How about you just wait a day and find out for yourself? Wait for sunset and get a good look at what she really is."

Violet's insides turned to tar. She stared at Truck's back so hard her eyes dried out. A convulsion ran over him, and the sight of it flayed the top layer off her heart. He finally turned to look at her fully, and the effort it cost him was staggering. His eyes were unreadable, hollowing Violet out completely.

As if that wasn't torture enough, her father started to laugh. A snide, triumphant trumpet soon joined by the rest of The Pack, glorying in her humiliation.

With a sudden snap of her limbs, Violet skittered back down the metal stairs. Her lungs burned as she kicked up sand in her flight across the courtyard. Crashing past the reinforced door to the barracks, she shoved her way inside.

The corridors were unlit, but her eyes adjusted quickly to the dark, and she fled through the warren of hallways to her room, slamming the door behind her. Her breath ran high and hysterical in her chest, but she was too threadbare to give over to tears.

All she wanted to do was claw up the floor, scratching away concrete and soil until she'd dug a grave to hide herself in.

But that wasn't in the fucking cards.

And it wouldn't have made a bit of difference anyhow. Her father was right – at sunset the next day, she'd turn into one of those horrid beasts and scrape her way back out again. If Truck was unlucky enough to be there when it happened, Violet wouldn't be able to stop herself from slaughtering him.

No, there was no other avenue open to her.

She had to leave.

Worst of all, she was going to have to go back to The Pack. Everything she'd done to try and save herself had been in vain. What made her sicker than anything else was the fact that she'd dragged Truck Laine into hell for nothing.

TWENTY

I've got to get the fuck out of here, *Truck thought.* Cut bait and save your own fucking neck while you can.

Damsel in distress? He could do that. Werewolves? Stickier to swallow, but bring it on. Violet being one of those... things? That just might be the interstate exit too far.

Truck wouldn't have put it past The Duke or any of the other despicable scoundrels in his entourage to lie about Violet. Top tier tactic, actually. He might even have laughed at it if she hadn't turned tail and fled. There was plenty Truck could rationalize away, but that was tantamount to a balls-front confession.

He'd put himself on the line for a goddamn Werewolf.

And not just any Werewolf – the daughter of the goddamn Wolf Man King. A girl who'd been hiding the truth from jump street. Stringing him along to save her own ass. Nice though that ass was, Truck had been used. Played for a sucker.

And he knew it.

He cursed himself that he hadn't caught on sooner. Every time he tried to pry the full story out of Violet, she'd evaded like the truth would scald the inside of her throat. No surprise considering the epic fucking shit she was keeping in her gut.

The trick was, Truck couldn't quite bring himself to hate her for it.

There was a thread of honest fear in her that he just couldn't shake off. Violet had spent most of her time in his company full-tilt terrified. Fear like that was hard to fake. There was no doubt in his mind that when he first saw her, Violet was running for her life. Werewolf or not, she was trying to escape the marauding band in hopes of... what, exactly?

Even if she managed to get somewhere The Pack would never be able to find her, that wouldn't change what she was.

If her father hadn't dimed her out, just what would have happened? Truck would've been locked in this fortress getting chased around by some slobber-mouthed demon until the sun came up.

Unless he had Pepper on hand... but the thought alone nauseated him so much he had to scream.

"Fuck!"

Any time Truck's mind got spinning like this, he knew what he needed to do – get his hands busy. And given his situation, there was one very clear way to do that.

Before The Duke and his merry men screeched back off towards the horizon, they made one thing perfectly clear. If it was up to them, Truck wasn't going to survive this. Maybe if he'd offered Violet up earlier they'd have let him walk away — but now that his clothes were stained with no-shit Werewolf blood, he was gonna have to pay.

Unless he could fight his way out.

So he sat at the workbench doing what he could to melt down silver and forge it into bullets. Nice as it would have been to bust out some nine millimeter hollow points to blast the whole mess of them to smithereens, he didn't have the skill.

Maybe if Dean was here.

Thinking of his friend's sacrifice tied Truck's windpipe in a knot. The poor dumb bastard had gone and gotten himself killed, and for what? Defending some girl he didn't even know? One who just so happened to be a super-secret Werewolf? Truck's fingers trembled so hard he dropped a casing and spilled gunpowder all over the workstation.

"Goddamnit," he muttered, laying his palms flat on the table top and sucking hard breaths in through his teeth. "Get yourself together."

The dense, heady stink of molten silver stung his nostrils, and he kicked on the exhaust fan. Its roaring drone helped to muffle the thoughts banging around in his skull, but only up to a point.

He and Dean hadn't seen much of each other in the last half decade, but they were linked. Joined forever by sorrow and loss. Now that Dean was gone, a gaping wound ruptured open right in the middle of Truck's life, spilling miserable pus all over everything. He's spent every day since the death of his sister trying to fill that bottomless pit with whatever he could find, and now there was no escaping it.

Maybe that's why he'd invested in Violet so deeply. She was the young woman he might actually be able to save, and every time he saw her in danger, all kinds of buried shit came roaring back from the grave.

There was no way the two of them could win against The Pack if it actually came to an all-out war. Truck needed to bow out and run while he had the chance. Because even if she hadn't been straight with him from the beginning, Truck knew there was no way he could just hang by and watch her die.

Violet had made it abundantly clear she'd rather be dead than fall back into the clutches of The Duke – let alone The Chamberlain and all his lust-fueled groping. As Truck's hands numbly resumed filling shotgun shells with powder and silver pellets, the bottom of his brain mulled over what Violet might do with one if she got a moment alone with Pepper.

He'd already tried to piece together the back of one girl's head, and he was in no hurry to go through that again.

"Hey." Violet's voice made Truck jump, and he regarded her slowly over his shoulder. She stood in the open doorway, looking smaller and more helpless than ever.

Try as he might, Truck couldn't make himself see the dark monster lurking under her skin. All he could see was a girl who needed his help. Not only that, her very presence tugged at his heart in a way that was impossible to ignore.

"Hey," he replied, turning back to the workbench. He couldn't look at her. It hurt too much. Best thing to do was keep grinding out shells. If Violet wanted a better answer than that, she was gonna have to work for it.

Which seemed like it might not pan out.

A long silence closed around them. Even though he didn't look back, Truck could feel her getting closer. The girl could move without making a sound, but that shimmery little glimmer grew in his chest until he was sure she was coming over. He knew she was at his side even before her slender hand landed on his shoulder.

"There are some things we need to talk about." Her voice was strong and fearful at the same time, and Trucks arms itched with the need to pull her close to him.

He resisted.

"I'd say so," he answered flatly. Pulling the crank to crimp the shell shut and secure the percussion cap, Truck kicked out another silver shot. Switching off the ventilator, he killed the flame under the crucible of melted silver, and turned to face her.

Half of him wanted to interrogate her. Just rake Violet over the coals and drag answers out by the root. But one look at her face and he couldn't do it. Her eyes were red from crying, and her skin pale with dread. How could he be anything other than gentle with this girl? Werewolf or not.

"Why?" he managed at last. "Why didn't you tell me?" Violet heaved a sigh so profound she almost rattled to pieces from it.

"I was afraid. I thought you'd turn your back on me, and I needed you so much." Her hands found his chest, and she searched his face with pitiful sincerity. "I still need you, Truck. More than I can ever say."

Her words loitered in the air, and Truck clenched his jaw to keep them from slipping down his throat. As mixed up as he was, Violet had just managed to say the one thing that could shake his resolve to leave.

"I'm going to need you to be honest with me," he said, forcing himself to pull away from her. "Because the truth has been in pretty short supply around here." Violet drew back, wounded. Everything in Truck screamed out to smooth things over. Just to touch her. But he folded his arms across his chest instead.

If there was witchcraft in this girl, he was gonna have to mind his Ps and Qs to keep from succumbing to it.

"You're right," she whispered. "I haven't done right by you. If you think you can forgive me, I'll do my best to tell you as much of the truth as I can. That's a promise." Truck didn't move a muscle, and his stern exterior shattered her composure. Violet's knees wobbled, and she visibly shook. Then, licking her lips, she asked meekly, "Is it alright if I sit down?"

Truck grunted and nodded to a couple of ammo boxes next to the work station. Violet perched on the edge of them, tangling her fingers in her lap.

"So, yes," she began. "The Duke is my father. And thanks to him, I'm..." she trailed off.

"One of those things," Truck finished for her. There wasn't any accusation in the way he said it, but she flinched anyway.

"Yes." Even knowing the answer was coming, it snatched Truck's breath right out of his lungs. Bracing his hands on his knees, he nodded slowly and stared at the slab floor.

"So, were you just going to wait?" he asked. "Hunker down in here with me until tomorrow night and then… what? Rip me up and run back out to join your *family*?"

"They are not my *family*," Violet bit back with startling ferocity. "I hate every last one of those gutless, despicable pieces of trash!" Her eyes flashed. "This isn't some elaborate trap I've laid, if that's what you're wondering."

"What is it then?" Truck didn't want to get heated, but tough shit. It was a heated situation. "What is all this?"

"My last chance," she wailed, robbing him of whatever outrage had started to climb up his spine. "In three days I'm cursed for life, and I just…" Her shoulders dropped, and she looked anywhere but Truck's face. "I didn't have a plan when I first ran away. I just knew I had to get out. I thought maybe something would happen to put an end to all this, but…" Her voice strangled up and she looked forlorn into the middle distance.

Truck considered her for a long moment, sizing it all up. There wasn't a whiff of a lie about her. He was the kind of guy who could smell dishonesty like a dead dog in the sun, and this girl was playing straight.

"What happens in three days?" he asked. Violet shook her head, bit her lower lip, then forced herself to meet his gaze.

"I turn twenty five," she said simply. "Once that happens, I'm stuck like this and there's no going back." A spark went off in the center of his chest and he rocked forward.

"But before that?" The way she hesitated at his question fanned that spark into a low flame. "Violet, are you saying there's a way back now?"

"Maybe." She looked into Truck's face so intently that it made his breath catch. "If someone afflicted with this can kill the person who infected them before their twenty-fifth birthday, the curse is broken."

"Meaning?" Truck's question drew a peculiar smile to her lips.

"I need to kill my father."

The words were simple, but a kind of mythic weight hung over them. Chance "The Duke" Summers was like a figure out of legend, carrying such an aura of eternal inevitability that Truck wondered if it was *possible* to kill him. At the same time, a row of silver packed shotgun shells by his side stood as a testament to the man's mortality.

"Hang on." Truck tightened his grip on his knees, hacking through the bramble bush in his brain. "You're saying your father *turned* you? Like, at some point your old man actually *bit* you to make you like him?"

Violet's chin scrunched into a peach pit and her cheeks paled.

"No. I was born like this."

"Well, then..." Truck huffed in a breath, flinging up his hands in exasperation.

"But my mother was human," Violet pressed on. "The Duke took her, and after I was born, he discarded her. Now that he had someone to carry on the bloodline, she wasn't worth anything to him."

"Discarded?" Truck asked cautiously. The girl in front of him fixed him with a resentful gaze.

"I think you know what I mean." The coldness of it whistled through the marrow of Truck's bones. This young woman was nowhere near as brittle as one might think. She'd seen more horrors in twenty four years to last until the end of time. Nobody should have to suffer the life she'd had.

"With your father gone, you think your mother's side of your nature will win out? This whole thing will just evaporate?"

"What other hope do I have?"

That knocked Truck back on his stool. Violet had nothing. In the whole spinning universe, she had one thread to cling onto, and it was frayed at both ends. Worse still, there were other dangers ready to snip it in the middle.

"And what about this Chamberlain asshole? Is that why The Duke wants you back so bad? Just so he can hand you off to that piece of shit?"

Violet snorted in disgust and shook her head.

"The Chamberlain doesn't matter to my father at all. I think if The Duke knew what his right hand man was trying to do to me, he'd gut him like a fish."

"Then why?" The question rippled up from Truck's chest like a storm. "If it's not about marrying you off, then what the fuck is all this about? Why is The Duke willing to burn the world down over this?"

"Because I'm *his*," she answered simply. "I'm of his blood. He owns me. And what The Duke owns, The Duke *keeps*." It sounded like the slamming of a prison door. Blood honor. Pride. Pure stubborn will. The only language brutes and tyrants understand. Now that he knew the full extent of the stakes, Truck looked the situation right in its stark face.

"I want to be perfectly clear," Truck said. "You're telling me if we can manage to take down The Duke, you won't be a Werewolf anymore?"

"Not *we*, Truck." There was an uncanny certainty in the way she put it that raised the hair on the back of his arms. "I can't ask you to risk yourself for that. I won't let you." Her reversal was so abrupt, so shocking that Truck's mouth fell open.

"Come again?"

"I've already put you in so much danger. Too much. It would be wrong of me to ask for more."

Truck's ears started ringing, and his pulse pounded in his temples until he thought his head would crack right down the middle.

"What are you saying?"

"I came to tell you I'm leaving."

Truck damn near had a stroke.

"You're fucking *what?*"

"If I stay, they'll kill you. Both of us, probably. So, I'm walking through those doors to do what I can on my own."

"Like hell you are!" He surged to his feet, every protective atom in his body sizzling. "I haven't come this far just for you to wave so-long and kick up your heels. Goddamnit, Dean Harrison didn't go and get himself killed just so you can pull some bullshit surrender game." His dead friend's name lodged in his throat, the only hiccup to let him know he was shouting full bore. Hackles up, red faced, and Violet shrank under the power of his fury.

"I'm not surrendering," she protested, but he was too hot to hear her.

"What do you call it, then? Because if you walk out there alone, it's game over."

"Truck, please—"

"Please *what*, Violet? Please stand here like a fucking sucker and lose everything? Lose *you?* I don't fucking think so!" He paced like a tiger on a hot plate, his fists clenched so tight he could have punched a hole in the sun.

"Lose me?" She repeated his own words back to him, and they singed his ear drums. In a heated moment, he'd betrayed a secret he was keeping even from himself. He opened his mouth to speak, then slammed it shut again.

"Forget it," he grumbled, retreating.

"I need to know, Truck." Violet touched his arm with such tenderness he was powerless to resist. When he met her eyes, they were wide, vulnerable, and most startling – *hopeful*. "Would losing me really be losing everything?"

The question snatched his heart and wouldn't let go. If he wasn't careful, he'd slip into a whole cauldron of shit he was nowhere near ready to deal with. Even if he wasn't faced with a battalion of storybook monsters made manifest, saying the words echoing in his blood would have been next to impossible.

"I need to think," Truck grunted at last.

"Truck?" She reached for him, but he was so fired up he batted her hand away.

"Just give me a second, will you? Can I get one fucking second?" Only when his throat throbbed did he realize how loud he was screaming. The fog in his eyes cleared and he looked to find Violet cowering in front of him. Her eyes were lined with tears again, and she held her hands up as if she thought he might strike her.

How could she think that of him?

The answer hit him like a bucket of cold water.

Because it's what she knows.

Misery dumped into his blood thick as tar. After everything she'd been through – that unfathomably brutal life she'd just spilled out before him – the idea that he could do anything to make her afraid of him was like a scorpion's nest in his heart.

Was he frustrated? Yes. Tangled up in a thousand miles of his own shit? Double yes. But to let her imagine for an instant he could take it out on *her*?

He could have dropped dead on the spot.

An agonizing howl ripped out of Truck's throat, and he broke for the door.

He needed air. He needed the hot sun on his skin. He needed one single thing in this whole unhinged world to make sense.

What he craved most was sanity, but the universe was fresh out.

To make matters worse, the sun was setting.

Just peeping over the rim of the compound, the nearly-full moon hung huge and low in the sky.

Waiting.

TWENTY-ONE

Truck stalked across the courtyard, and Violet's heart wilted with every step he took.

What just happened?

She'd made up her mind to put on her big girl panties and fend for herself, but now the absurd peril of it all nailed her feet to the ground. Every inch of her cried out to run after Truck and make things right – she just wasn't sure how exactly they'd gone wrong. All she'd tried to do was save him, and he'd screamed the place down.

As if that wasn't enough, he'd confessed something that made her insides ring like a bell.

Did I hear him right?

He said that losing me would be like losing everything.

In the deepest parts of her gut she'd dared to hope as much, but hearing it out loud was something else altogether. Even if it was a slip of the tongue on his part.

The truth has a way of sneaking out when people aren't thinking too hard about what they're saying. Which begged an even larger question. One she'd been trying like hell to keep from asking herself, but it kept getting trickier and trickier to avoid.

Now there was no getting around it.

Just what do I feel for him?

He'd saved her life more than once, sticking out his neck so far it was a miracle nobody had ridden by to slash it.

Not that they hadn't tried.

On top of all that, he'd shown her that there were heights of pleasure she'd never dreamed existed. For the first time in her life, her body wasn't a stranger to her.

Most of the time it felt like her biggest enemy. But new horizons spread out before her, promising that her body was so much more than a cage. Under the right care, it might just turn out to be a garden.

She had Truck to thank for that.

It was a terrible gift.

Ever since she was a little girl, Violet lived in fear of the ferocious animal her skin kept hidden. But Truck had thrown back the curtain on an even more savage, ravenous devil in her blood, who craved love more than violence. It demanded meals of limitless pleasure and true affection.

And the only food it would accept was Tucker Laine.

"Shit," she mumbled, slumping against the workbench. A handful of shells tipped over and rolled along the worn wooden top.

What had she been thinking? Had she been thinking at all?

A clatter in the courtyard drew her attention and Violet crept over to the door. Truck had his knapsack out, cramming it with supplies under the rapidly purpling sky.

Shit.

Was he really going to leave her?

Just imagining it left her more bereft than she had ever been. More than when she'd first fled into the midnight desert praying for salvation. Deliverance skidded up on eighteen wheels, and now it was about to roll right back out of her life.

Isn't that what she'd asked for? Whether he left her or she left him, wasn't it all the same in the end?

Maybe it would have been – before he revealed how he really felt. Even in the face of knowing what she was. He'd learned her most private shame, and cared for her anyway. Now that there were no more secrets between them, parting ways had to be impossible. Yet there he was, equipping his rig, his face set with grim determination.

"I can't," she whispered to herself. "I can't let him go out after dark. They'll kill him if he does."

Night thickened around them more every second, and if Truck breached that gate, it would be thicker with his blood. Violet shut her eyes tight to banish the image, and a new resolution coalesced in her veins.

She wasn't going to let Truck become an unwitting sacrifice on the altar of her father's hatred. If anybody was baring themselves to the knife, it was going to be her.

Truck's back was to her, and Violet took her opportunity. Scampering like a coked up jackrabbit, she made straight for the front gates. Gazing up at the heavy bolt, she knew there was no fastening it behind her. All she could do was pray that Truck had the presence of mind to do it before hell came stealing in to find him.

Or maybe he would slide behind the wheel and barrel off in the opposite direction to live another day. Either way, Violet's mind was made up. It was a frying pan or fire moment, and she was gonna try her luck with the flaming coals.

Fingering the grip, she tried to slide the bolt back as quietly as possible. It squeaked as she lifted the handle, and she shot a cringing glance Truck's way.

He hadn't heard.

Violet gave the bolt a solid tug… and it didn't budge. Her pulse skyrocketed. She worked it back and forth, risking grating noises as she tried to wrest it free. But she was learning fast that opening thirty foot high steel gates without making a sound was a fool's errand.

Shit was getting noisy whether she liked it or not.

It was strategy time.

Wedging herself into a corner, she held her breath and waited for Truck to go back inside. He was going to have to, right? Even if it was just for one last piss before cranking Layla's engine.

His temper must have slowed because he wasn't haphazardly jamming things in his pack anymore. Truck moved thoughtfully, almost methodically as he checked and rechecked to make sure everything was in place. This was the careful Truck she had come to know. Beyond all the snap decisions and rough-and-tumble was a man of deep consideration.

Violet trembled all over with how much she longed for him. She chewed her knuckles to keep from crying his name and running into his arms to try and make everything right. But that would be a trap of the worst kind – one she set for herself. So she sat in the dirt and watched him, drinking in his every move so she could remember him as clearly as possible for whatever shred of life awaited her.

At last, he turned and headed back for the barracks. Since she was lapping him up anyway, she let herself admire every scrumptious bit of his body as he walked. The sway of his shoulders, the strut in his hips, and the curve of his ass.

If this was her last look, she was going to make the by-god most of it. Then he vanished through the doorway, and there was no denying it any longer.

This is a man worth dying for.

Which meant it was go time.

Leaping up, she seized the bolt and pulled with all her might. It ground free with a cast iron wail that rattled her bones, then rang the door like a gong as it lurched to a stop.

If Truck had been stone deaf and on the moon, he couldn't have missed it.

Violet flashed her attention to the open barracks doorway, and sure as shit, Truck poked his head out. Their eyes locked for less than a second before she hauled the door open and wriggled through the crack.

Night slammed around her as she sprinted into the open.

Here she was again.

Alone.

Just her and the desert, and the wild lack of a plan. So much had changed since she first left The Pack, and yet she was right back where she started.

Her limbs stretched with her determination to put as much distance as possible between herself and the man she was trying to save. In no time, her lungs thrummed with icy pain, and her joints burned, ready to splinter.

A headlamp blazed to life, stopping Violet in her tracks. Then another. And another. Headlight after headlight hacked into the dark, imprisoning Violet in a circle of repulsive yellow eyes. She shielded her face with her arm, staggering in an unsteady circle like a newborn fawn.

Figurative lamb to the literal slaughter.

An engine sputtered to terrible life, and Violet's skin exploded into gooseflesh. She would have known the sound of her father's mount as surely as she knew the trick of his voice.

The Chamberlain's bike snarled up next, followed by Scum, and soon the whole greasy chorus threatened to deafen her. Violet clamped her hands over her ears, screaming to try and drown out the chaotic tapestry that had been the backdrop of her entire life. She opened her throat and howled until tears scalded down her cheeks. All at once, the engines cut and the terrible prairie silence swept in to throttle her.

Violet's knees gave way and she crumbled to the ground,

sobbing over great fistfuls of soil. Tears spattered down, and the thirsty earth drank them so fast they almost hissed into steam.

"What are you crying for, Vee?" Her father stepped from his saddle, coming around until his detestable silhouette blotted out his headlight. "That human back there?"

"Let him live," she gasped, only to be met with a nasty chuckle.

"What for?" The question hovered for a moment, then his tone shifted into pure mockery. "Oh. I see." He ambled closer to crouch in front of her. "Did you go and get sweet on him? Is that what happened?" Low, lascivious laughter bubbled up from the darkness behind the high beams. Violet's stomach heaved knowing every man among them was picturing her in the throes of passion.

"Don't," she spat.

"Don't what?" The Duke taunted. When her fury kept her from answering immediately, he leaned so close she could smell the sweat reeking in his clothes. "Come on. Don't what, Vee?"

"Don't call me Vee!" Violet's spine unfurled and she rocked back onto her haunches to vent her outrage at the cold stars in the pitiless sky. Her father cooed with mockery as she wailed, but when he reached for her, Violet slapped his hand away. "Don't touch me! Not one of you, do you hear me?"

"Not even me?" Without having to see his face, Violet could hear the vile, lecherous smile on The Chamberlain's lips. It was all she could do not to retch so much they'd all be swept away on a river of bile. She went to speak, but something else bellowed up from within her. A feral, untamable roar erupted from her throat until her jaw ached.

"There it is." The Duke rose to his feet, looking down on her with fatherly approval. "There *you* are. I've been waiting for you to come back to yourself. Come on, darling. It's time to go home."

"No!" Much as she tried to shake it, the Wolf within her refused to loosen its grip. Her voice teetered perilously on the edge of the beast. Violet clamped her jaws together, straining to keep her teeth from sharpening. She looked at her hands, and thick hair snaked out of her skin.

"Don't fight it," The Duke whispered. "It's who you are."

"No," she shrieked again, and it elongated into a lonesome, miserable howl. Others rose to meet it, stifling Violet with shame. She reached deep into herself to drag humanity up by the heels. The sweet, tender girl she guarded in the center of her heart swam to the surface, driving the Wolf off her skin.

"What are you doing?" her father demanded as her body smoothed again. "Stop it!"

"Never again," Violet gulped, her voice her own.

"Tomorrow night," The Duke shouted. "Tomorrow night!" His own voice melted into lupine gravel, his eyes yellowing as he returned to the monstrous shape he gloried in. "You can resist now, but when the moon is full, there's no hiding what you are."

"Why would you want this for me? This... this *curse*?" A cowed murmur swept through the onlookers. Among The Pack, that was a forbidden word. Anyone who dared utter *curse* was met with brutal punishment.

The Duke's lips curled away from his teeth, and his long tongue flicked between them as he regarded his daughter before him in the dust. Violet had seen every shade of her father's wrath, but this was something new.

"Never say that." It wasn't a warning. It was a command from the mountaintop. "This is no curse. It's a *calling*. We can't be men because we shame to be men. But us?" He spread his arms to the citizens of his ragtag empire. "Our line stretches back to antiquity. You, my daughter, are descended from the ancient Gods. The ones who ruled before civilization made kings cowards. Who would surrender that legacy to live like *men*?"

"I would." She got to her feet, squaring up in defiance. "Gladly."

"A daughter of mine?" The Wolf stole deeper into his voice. Any shred of humanity whistled away until Violet saw nothing she could call a father.

"Never."

The Duke reared back, his chest swelling at the sky as he sucked in a powerful breath, then let fly with a howl so rich and terrible that no one dared to join in. This was the call of an elder god loosed upon the Earth.

When his gaze returned to her again, Violet saw nothing but hell.

A swipe sent her sprawling backwards to tumble on the hard ground. Her head rang, and the coppery taste of her own blood filled her mouth. She blinked for a moment, her cheek stinging to life from the force of his blow.

Rolling onto her back, she stared up at the monster advancing on her with deliberate steps. She scrambled away from him, but when she tried to get up The Duke planted a boot on her shoulder and shoved her down again. The Chamberlain revved his bike, and soon all the others followed suit, cheering on the gladiatorial lashing unfolding in the center of their headlight Colosseum.

The Beast, formerly known as The Duke, roared low in her face, flecks of spittle plastering her cheeks as her hair blew back. He lifted his paw again, arcing wide to deliver a punishing strike. Violet cringed and readied to take the blow, but a gunshot punched a hole in the night.

Her father's throaty rumble withered into an agonized wheeze, and when she opened her eyes, he was clutching his wrist hard. A pulpy mess dripped from where his hand should be, sizzling bubbles of gore slopping down his arm.

The Duke doubled over, clamping down to keep fetid black blood from spurting in every direction.

"Silver," one of The Pack cried. Another gunshot sent them ducking over their bikes, skittering off in every direction to save their miserable, flea-bitten asses.

Only The Duke remained, looking from his smoking stump to his daughter with all the hatred the Devil keeps locked up. Then with a single bound, he straddled his chopper and zigzagged into the darkness.

Violet twisted in place, and there was Truck. The shock sight of him almost overwhelmed her with relief.

He was so close, it was a saint-making miracle none of The Pack had seen him coming. But they'd been too distracted by wholesale female carnage to see much beyond the tips of their dreadful dicks.

"You wounded him," Violet said as Truck pulled her to her feet.

"Too bad. I was trying to decapitate the son of a bitch." He tucked a strand of hair behind her ear, and soothed her aching cheek with his palm. "I'll get him next time."

"Next time?"

"I couldn't let you go." He looked into her face with enough love to topple mountains. "And I could never leave you. Let's get you inside. We've got work to do." Violet held him in place.

"Just a second."

Truck looked at her confused.

"They won't stay gone for long," he said.

"Long enough for this." Violet got on her toes and kissed him. It might just wind up being the last kiss they ever shared, so she wanted to be sure it counted.

Wasting kisses was out of the question, especially with nine circles of hell on the way.

TWENTY-TWO

Truck charged into the armory like he was storming the beach at Normandy. Violet wasn't far behind him, and when she came up next to him he could tell she knew how bleak their prospects were. In terms of shit to take down The Pack, there wasn't much to look at.

"How many silver shells do we have?" she asked.

"About a dozen." Truck set his jaw, swallowing against the knot in his gullet. "That ain't gonna be enough, is it?" Violet hugged up to his arm, her fearful expression telling him he was bang on the money.

"Even with a couple of lucky shots, that's nowhere near enough to take out all of them," she said dismally. All Truck could do was nod.

"I figured." Riding in like a hero was nice and all, but only if you had what it takes to put a win over the plate. The lack of Werewolf-killing ammo might not have been Truck's fault, but he was the one stuck with the bill.

"How quickly can we make more?"

Her answer came in the form of howls and screaming engines. They didn't have the time to spit, let alone pump out shells. Dean cranked rounds of ammo like a machine, but he was out of the picture.

"We need to think outside the box. Fast." Truck looked around hoping for anything to spark his imagination, but came up empty handed – until his eyes landed on the scattering of silver Dean had dragged out to melt down. "Huh."

"What?"

"Dean was a prepper of the first order."

"Meaning?"

Truck swiveled to face her, hopeful they could make a banquet out of this crumb of good news. "Meaning, what we're looking at here doesn't even *touch* the silver he's got stashed away in this place. Wait 'til you see what he's got squirreled back."

He started rummaging across the workbench, driven by the sound of Satan's army tearing ass around outside the walls. His fingers finally brushed a jingling key ring, and he all but did a backflip.

"Paydirt," he grunted in satisfaction, then grabbed Violet's hand. "Come on." Shit was loud while they were in the armory, but when they were back out in the open, it was just this side of balls-out mayhem.

"Jesus Christ," Violet whimpered.

"Worse than usual?"

"I've never heard them like this."

"They've got a fresh reason for some bloodlust. After blasting pappy's paw, they're gonna double down on cracking this egg and scrambling us good."

Violet quaked, but Truck suspected what he just said had fuckall to do with it. There was one animal cry louder than the rest, whistling over the top of the insanity like a soprano in a country choir.

"That's him, isn't it? Your father?"

She nodded, her face so pale the skin was translucent. The bald terror fired Truck up even more, and he made a beeline directly for his late pal's plunder hut.

"What are you doing," she asked as Truck started thumbing through the keys. He could blame her being confused. The tiny above ground shack had all the trappings of manufactured ramshaklendom. Only a sharpest eye would notice the edges were reinforced with steel plates. Smears of paint, motor oil, and piles of ragged tires might have fooled the casual observer, but Truck knew Dean better than that. This shanty might as well have a neon sign reading, "Nothing To See Here."

"Damnit," he muttered, trying every key on the ring as the fury beyond the gate reached its zenith. Just when Truck thought it was a loser's proposition, the lock turned and the door swung open. The smell of kerosene and money wafted up the spiral staircase, and Truck grinned when he hit the light switch.

"You've gotta be shitting me," Violet muttered, gobsmacked at the sight of so much wealth. Truck had seen it before himself, and it was still enough to blow his hair back.

Heaps of golden artifacts climbed out of steamer trunks. Ropes of pearls hung from everything, studded with sapphires and rubies the size of apricots. And that was just a peek from the top of the stairs.

They trundled down the steps, astonished as a slapped ass by the sprawling hoard. Not just gold and jewels, but artwork, Persian rugs, fine furniture, and pallets stacked with good old US greenbacks. There was enough treasure here to make Blackbeard's dick hard for a thousand years.

"What did I tell you?" Truck quipped over his shoulder. "My boy Dean's been busy."

Nice as it might have been to get all Scrooge McDuck and plunge in for a jolly swim, their most precious commodity was dwindling fast – time.

"Over there!" Violet must have been able to sniff out silver a mile away because she dashed over to a heap of candlesticks and gleaming flatware spilling out of a

Chippendale armoire. They swung the doors wide, and were met with glittering mounds of Kennedy half dollars, Roosevelt dimes, Washington Quarters – a whole host of silver coins with dead presidents stamped on their shiny asses.

Ingots were good for melting down, but this stuff was far more in line with what Truck had in mind.

"Let's load up." Truck grabbed a duffel bag and they scooped armloads of money into its waiting gullet. "Silverware next," he said after all the coins were accounted for. "Keep it small."

"What are you planning?"

"A nasty surprise."

By the time Truck figured they had enough, the satchel was so heavy he had to lug it upstairs one step at a time. With every heave the noise got louder. Down in that treasure pit, he could almost forget the savagery they had to face down.

The place had walls thick enough to withstand a goddamn nuclear holocaust, and was stuffed to the gills with riches. A lesser man might have tried to lock them into that cellar to weather the storm, but Truck wasn't that brand of chump.

You can't boil down gold and make soup.

Truck dragged the silver stash into the center of the courtyard, then rolled over an empty oil drum and kicked off the lid. That done, he bolted back into the armory and shouldered a nail keg full of black powder.

Violet watched him with pensive attention, gnawing her lower lip. Truck thumped the keg down at her feet.

"Dump this in," he told her. "Then put down a layer of silver. I'd say cutlery first. I'll grab some more powder." He turned to head back into the armory, but she caught him by the arm, arresting his step.

"Truck, wait."

"Time's tight, Violet. What's up?"

"I love you."

Those three little words grabbed his heart like a rabbit and ran off into the bushes. Truck almost tipped over, his head spinning so fast he couldn't hear the marauders anymore. There was nothing but her.

"Say that again?"

"I love you, Truck. More than anything."

"But…" He struggled to get his head straight. "Why tell me now?"

"The chances of us making it out of this are slim. I just need you to know in case we don't survive."

Truck launched himself at her, sweeping her off her feet and smothering her against his chest. She was so fragile in his arms – so small – yet her courage to come right out and say that to him made her mightier than Queen Kong.

"No one has ever made me feel the way you do." His voice was tight around the jagged lump in his throat. "You're… everything. And I can't lose you."

"Truck."

"You don't understand." He set her down, cradling her face in his hands as the tempest battered at the gates. "I just lost one of my oldest friends. The only link I had to my sister. I can't keep losing the people I love the most." It was a clumsy way of saying it back to her, but it was the best he could do in the moment.

"You won't lose me," she assured him. "You can't." Her hand on his arm told him she'd heard what he meant to say more than the graceless words that stumbled out of his mouth. "I promise. If we go down, then we're going down together."

She was right. Whatever happened, their futures were linked even until death. He kissed her, and his lips made every promise his words had failed to find.

"Alright," he said when he drew back. "I'm getting more gunpowder. Once this fucker's filled up," he kicked the side of the drum, "it's showtime."

TWENTY-THREE

The churning fog of dust was so thick at the top of the wall it nearly choked her, but Violet filled her lungs and shouted with all her might.

"Get your hands off me!" Despite her protestations, Truck grappled with her arms, holding her tight and shaking her to beat the band.

"Listen to me, goddamnit!"

"No!" She wrenched herself free and took off along the catwalk, hurtling to the far corner. Some of the bikes below slowed, bunching together with their glittering eyes turned upward. The Pack was jammed tighter than a hornet's nest, their idling bikes rumbling underneath the argument spilling out overhead.

Truck was on her again, pinning Violet to the railing and ravaging her neck with brutal kisses. His stubble raked her skin red, raising nasty grumbles from the Wolf Men. Violet shoved his chest to free herself, but in doing so almost fell backwards over the railing. Startled cries rose up to meet her, spiking until she righted herself.

"Get away from me!" She cracked Truck across the face with a slap so wicked her palm would sting for a week.

Truck's head snapped from the blow, and when he looked back at her his eyes were dark.

"You're going to regret that, you little *bitch*!"

"Is that all you think I am?" She lowered her chin, glaring at him with an evil grin. "Just a *little* bitch? You want to see just how *big* of a bitch I can be?" Somewhere deep inside, the padlock fell away from the cage, and the Wolf raged into her blood.

Run, Truck. Please.

It was agony to think of him seeing her like this, but there was no alternative. The Pack *had* to see her shift on him. After the way she'd fought against the monster inside her, they needed to watch her turn all that primal hatred against the man locked away with her. It was the only way to make The Pack believe the lie Violet and Truck needed them to swallow.

Violet's joints crackled as her body reformed itself. Delicious pain spread through her bones as the evil within her swelled to the surface. Each snap, each hateful rip of sinew feeding the rising demon under her skin.

The agony ran deeper than her body. Baring this part of herself to Truck was uglier than the deepest circles of hell. Her ultimate sacrifice to save their necks.

Truck's eyes flickered in disbelief, then terror. Her heart shattered for what he witnessed, but the spinning in her gut bled into a whirlwind. The edges of her vision thickened as more and more of her animal self shoved its way through her.

Unfeigned fear rippled over Truck's face, then he did the thing he'd refused to do from the moment Violet laid eyes on him. Maybe the thing he should have done all along.

He ran.

Turned on his heel and charged along the catwalk for the ringing metal staircase. Cheers erupted from the hairy spectators as she bounded after him. This was what they wanted all along, and the parts of Violet that hadn't quite dissolved yet curdled up in shame for giving it to them. Even if it was a ruse.

When she reached the ground, Violet was struggling to keep herself in check. Out of the sight of The Pack, she battled to regain control. To tip the balance in favor of humanity. Otherwise things could get out of hand in ways that she would never recover from.

Thankfully for her, Layla was already running. The door hung open, but the driver's seat was empty. Truck was still on foot, and Violet forced herself to lope along in a wide arc, hugging the wall to keep from getting close to him. There was no telling what might happen if she did. Actually, there was all kinds of telling what would happen, and every story was a bad one.

Truck jerked back the bolt barring the gates, and the devil between Violet's ribs shrieked how near Truck was to freedom. Violet chased him around the cab as more and more of her barbarous side surged for control.

Truck only just managed to climb into the cab, jerking his door shut so fast it almost bit Violet's fingers.

Jamming it in gear, Truck blew through the open gates, black exhaust billowing out of his stacks. Without the trailer to slow things down, the vehicle was a seven ton battering ram.

The last thing Violet saw before he vanished into the smoke was a motorcycle strapped to the back of the cab. Violet knew it well, and the human part of her prayed The Pack would be too drunk with victory to notice one of their own bikes playing stowaway.

The bike's engine was already running, sputtering in impotent desperation to be free. For now it was Layla's sole cargo – but its time would come.

With Truck out of arm's reach, Violet's humanity battled bitterly against the snapping jaws of her curse, refusing to back down. She'd denied it with every scrap of her being, and now that it was so close to the surface it demanded release.

But she wasn't giving up.

Not even as The Pack swarmed through the doors, thundering like a beehive full of chainsaws. Stinking exhaust snaked into her lungs, gorging her internal enemy. Resisting the animal call to surrender, Violet beat back against it, finally mastering herself before falling to the ground in a bone weary heap.

All that did was whip The Pack into a greater frenzy. The cacophony reached skull splitting levels as motor rips echoed over each other off the walls, spiraling so high heaven itself seemed ready to crack.

Violet lay at the center of this diabolical hurricane, counting the bikes until she was certain every living member of The Pack was accounted for. Then she hauled herself to her feet and cried out until the veins in her neck were ready to burst.

One by one the riders skidded to a stop, every furious eye bent on her tiny, human frame. Out of the earthy haze stepped her father in Half-Wolf form. Black blood soaked through the tattered flannel shirt tied around his stump. The Duke advanced on her, undisguised cruelty dripping from his lips.

"Silver shot?" he roared. "You gave that fucker *silver shot?*"

"I didn't give him *anything,*" she spat back. "He and his friend Dean made it after they found out what *you* are." She sneered in a circle, making damn sure every member of The Pack felt her searing contempt.

"How many does he have," The Duke demanded. "Tell me." He took her by the throat, the tips of his claws piercing her skin.

"I don't know," she wheezed. "We weren't exactly on speaking terms when he took off." The Duke dropped her with a growl, and dusty air grated into her lungs.

"You should have killed him when you had the chance." Glaring down at her, his disgust was palpable. "You *finally* have the guts to return to your truest self, and you let him slip through your fingers?" Snorting his derision, he turned away. "Disgraceful." Presenting himself to his men, he commanded, "Get ready to roll out."

"He took them with him," Violet said, stopping The Duke in his tracks. "Whatever silver he had he put in the truck. In case you followed him."

"Oh, we're following him, alright. After I take care of you." Chance Summers squared up in front of his daughter. The vestiges of humanity in his features melted as the beast took over. His shoulders swelled until the seams of his leather vest started to rip. The tattoos covering his bare arms vanished under a dense thicket of greying fur.

The rest of The Pack followed suit, descending into the most terrifying versions of themselves. Any normal person would have perished for fear, and even though she had seen it all before, Violet quaked at the unholy terror of it.

God turned a blind eye on moments like this. Here was no room for the divine – the underworld was in full sway.

The Duke reveled in her distress, tipping back his head to howl at the nearly-full moon. His chest heaved, and he cut loose again, baying out his triumph. His minions raised their voices alongside his, bellowing over each other until the wrought iron walls shook.

When her father turned his bloodshot eyes back on her, Violet had no doubt what he intended to do. Chance Summers was going to make her pay for what she'd put him through. Every dead member of The Pack was coming out of her hide, and she'd bear the scars of his wrath until judgement day. She could already smell the blood on his hateful breath.

But a new sound sliced through the air with surgical speed. The Pack all stood astride their machines, motors rumbling in stillness, but a lone engine squealed full throttle.

The Duke blinked in confusion, turning his attention to the gates yawning just behind him. Out of the night came Truck, enthroned on the ride of their fallen comrade. In one hand he brandished a bottle with a rag stuffed in the neck, and only an idiot wouldn't see where the night was headed. Cracking out his zippo as he wove through the dumbfounded cretins, Truck lit the soaking fuse and juddered to a standstill directly beside Violet.

She lofted into the saddle behind him and looked her father dead in the eye.

"Do it."

"So long, fuckers!" Truck hurled the Molotov cocktail at the oil drum pipe bomb they'd made and hightailed it the fuck out of there. A cry went up, but it was too late.

A cosmic boom detonated into the night, piercing Violet's eardrums and rattling the flesh off her bones. Explosions cascaded over each other as their Fourth of July Silver Party wiped The Pack off the face of the planet with one staggering blow. Mother Earth was going to have a bruise for the next thousand years after a wallop like that.

Violet looked over her shoulder as ash and sparks rained down from the sky. A mushroom cloud bloomed over the compound, laced with white-hot flames. The doors were blown off, revealing an open furnace, blazing like Dante's own inferno.

A lone silhouette blotted out the flames. A hulking figure gunning his hellish steed, pursuing them like a soul let loose from the deepest pits of hell. The shoulders of his vest smoldered, smoke billowing off his back as he rocketed after them at top speed.

That bomb might have decimated The Pack, but there was one lone Wolf Rider left.

And she knew exactly who it was.

TWENTY-FOUR

The Duke.

Leave it to that bastard to get out of there in one piece. Well, mostly one piece. Truck smirked to himself that there was less of him now than when he woke up that morning. If Truck had his way, The Duke would never see another sunrise.

Violet tightened her grip around Truck's waist, lifting from the seat to put her mouth next to his ear.

"He's gaining fast."

"I know it." Truck let go of the handle bars just long enough to pat her thigh. "We just need to get to the rig. Once we're in there, he doesn't stand a chance."

Against two dozen mounted fiends, something Layla's size could be a liability. But against a lone rider? They could squash The Duke like a bug, then double back to let silver put the hound dog down for good.

Layla sat a few hundred yards away, doors open and waiting.

Problem was — the purloined bike was fast, but The Duke's was faster.

Before Truck and Violet were close enough to safely ditch

the motorcycle and clamber into the cab, the Werewolf was on them.

Truck cut to the side in an arc designed to lead The Duke away from Layla. The monster followed, but maybe a little too well for Truck's liking. Decades on two wheels gave The Duke the edge in this little game. Gunning in a tighter turn, the scoundrel managed to pull up alongside his quarry. Truck looked his way, and The Duke gnashed his teeth in anger.

They were close enough that Truck could see it wasn't just hot coals steaming from The Duke's back. His vest was littered with fragments of silver, and even boasted a couple of half dollars jutting out. A twisted fork lodged in the upper shoulder, and Truck grinned to think of the misery their little gambit had inflicted on the prick.

The Duke snarled, then whirled his arm over his head a few times. In a flash, Truck realized the fucker wielded a hefty length of chain. It was a marvel to see him steer with his stump while the other arm prepared for a top shelf thrashing.

"Brace yourself," Truck shouted, and The Duke let fly with his chain link bullwhip. It was a near miss – so close Truck could hear the blood in the air. The brute roared and readied to lash out again. Truck tried to put distance between them, but The Duke rolled so close Truck could smell singed dog hair and the stink of burning flesh.

This time the chain slithered across the front of the bike, shattering the headlight and sweeping up to belt Truck in the chest before raking off into darkness. Truck bit down hard, the vicious sting whistling through his body. If it had been a foot higher, it would have cleaved him right in half. As it was, it just ripped his shirt open and gave him some pretty gnarly cuts.

The Duke bellowed with venomous laughter at Truck's pain. His eyes glinted red with diabolical glee. An ugly grin cut a jagged line beneath his snout as he readied for another swing.

"You know what? Fuck this."

Truck wasn't going to give the shitheel another shot. If he was getting knocked off the bike, you can bet your mom's tits it was gonna be on his own terms.

Truck tossed a, "Hang on," over his shoulder, and rammed his front wheel directly into The Duke's. The Werewolf's eyes bulged in surprise, and the whole trio cartwheeled off the bikes into the scrub.

They landed in a tangle of limbs with The Duke at the bottom of the literal dog pile. After making sure Violet landed safely, Truck took advantage of the surprise by hauling off and planting a fist straight in The Duke's nose. There was a crunch of bone, and bright blood shot all over the place, but Truck had already pulled back to deliver another powerful punch. When it landed, The Duke wheezed through cracked, reddened teeth.

Then he started to laugh. The sound turned Truck's blood into snow broth.

"I have to hand it to you, truck driver. You're full of surprises."

Blows aside, The Duke was mastering himself again.

Falling off a bike and taking a sock in the jaw had to be the bread and butter of his life, and Truck knew not to push his luck. He hopped back and ran for his downed bike. Pepper was holstered to the side, and he seized her by the butt and wheeled around to end this rodeo.

"Truck, look out!"

Not only was The Duke on his feet again, but the chain was unfurling mid-air. Truck leaped back, but The Duke's whip wrapped around the shotgun and plucked it from his hands. Now that silver shot was out of the equation, Truck braced himself to do some hard math.

First order of business – he had to get close enough the

chain wasn't a viable weapon. If he couldn't have his gun, there was no way Truck was letting that piece of shit have the high ground.

With an open throated cry, Truck ducked low and rushed his opponent. Coming in shoulder first, he caught The Duke square in the middle of his chest. It was like charging into a brick wall. The masonry was shitty enough The Duke staggered back a step or two, but Truck got screwed in the bargain.

He hadn't broken his shoulder, but he hadn't done it any favors either.

The Duke got his breath back first and swiped the air with his claws. Truck managed to avoid getting nicked, but only just.

When it came to the heel of The Duke's boot, he wasn't so lucky. It smacked into Truck's ribs, and he collapsed with a grunt. Pain seared through him so far his grandkids were going to feel it.

Even with his descendants hanging in the balance, Truck's only thoughts were for Violet. After all, she had a stake in those little rugrats.

Rugwolves?

The Duke landed another brutal kick in Truck's side, and all thought of future generations faded. This shit was ending tonight. Too bad for Truck, he was on the losing end of things.

Turning to Violet in a daze, he saw her face had gone chalky white.

"Run," he grimaced to her. "Save yourself." She hesitated, and he sucked in as much air as his aching body could stand. "GO!"

A look of sorrow washed over her, then she pivoted and dashed for one of the downed bikes. As she hauled it up, her father looked after her with a curious, snickering pride. He waved her off, then came to stand over Truck.

"I have to hand it to you, truck driver," he said. "You put up one hell of a fight." The Duke was in his Half-Wolf state again, and reached up to yank the fork out of his shoulder. "And you know how to hit a guy where it hurts. Turning Violet against her old man the way you did? That's the work of a real fucker, you know that?"

"Takes one to know one," Truck grimaced.

"True." The Duke put his boot on Truck again and shoved him to his back. "But I was born this way. A leopard can't change his spots. Or something like that." He peeled off his vest, growling as the bits of silver lodged in it dug out of his flesh. The odor of burnt meat intensified, and hissing pops chased threads of smoke into the air.

The chopper kicked up, and Truck lifted his chin enough to see Violet peel out.

She didn't even look back.

"The desert is a hard place, truck driver. A cruel mistress. I don't expect you to understand this, but to survive out here, one *has* to be part animal. Man wasn't cut out for this. You're living proof of that right now, aren't you? In a couple of minutes, you'll be dead proof of that." He grinned. "Ain't that something?"

"Just do it," Truck scowled. If Violet was gone, then he wanted to turn out the lights as fast as possible.

"Oh, yeah?" A villainous chuckle curled past The Duke's lupine lips. "You think you're calling the shots, tough guy? Let me tell you something." He took a step forward, towering over Truck. "In this desert, I am the angel of death. Not only do I decide when something dies, I decide how long it takes. So." He rose to his full height. "Buckle up, truck driver. It's gonna be a long ride."

A gunshot split the night, and The Duke's back arched, his mouth open in a silent scream, eyes bulging in disbelief. Truck looked past him to see Violet standing with Pepper on her hip. The barrel smoked, and Violet wore an expression of pitiless satisfaction.

The Duke croaked, body stiff with pain. Truck figured he'd take things up a notch and kick The Duke square in the balls. The Werewolf hit his knees with a high whine, then squawked again as he rolled onto his bloodied, mashed up back.

Truck lurched to his feet and joined Violet in staring down at her father writhing in the dust.

"You came back," Truck said.

"I never left." Violet nudged him with her elbow, and Truck laid a hand on her shoulder. She may have been slight, but her whole being vibrated with power. They both gazed at the rasping, bloodied titan at their feet.

"What do you say we let him live?"

Violet screwed her mouth to the side and looked down at the quivering mess that was once at her father.

"Hmm."

The Duke's jaw worked, but all that came out was a lap of blood and some gurgling noises. Not exactly articulate, but his eyes pleaded with them for mercy.

"Nah."

Violet pulled the trigger, and blasted her dad straight to hell where he belonged.

THE CLOSER

With the Werewolf King done for, Violet and Truck took their damn sweet time heading back to the compound to take out any stragglers. Half of Scum clawed at the ground, dragging himself through the gate trailing intestines and bits of fur.

When Truck put Pepper's barrel in his mouth, the mangy piece of shit almost smiled.

What was left of The Chamberlain lay slumped against the back wall of the courtyard, about six dollars' worth of change embedded in his chest and skull. He was about as dead as a Werewolf was likely to get, but that didn't stop Violet from delivering a series of vicious kicks to the balls just for good measure.

"What do you think?" Truck asked after they'd taken accounts. "We get 'em all?"

"Every last one." The words came out like a sigh, and her shoulders dropped for the first time in her entire life.

I'm free.

They climbed back into Layla, and Truck cranked the girl to life. When he didn't immediately put it in gear, Violet looked his way.

"Is something wrong?"

"No, I was just thinking." A lazy smile danced across his lips. "We ought to do something nice for ourselves."

"Like?"

"Well." He put it in drive. "What if we went and hooked up the trailer? Then we come back and empty Dean's treasure stash into my girl here." Truck patted the dashboard. "If there's room, maybe we could plunder the armory a bit too."

"Just in case?"

"Just in case."

Violet eased back in her seat, stretching her arms over her head and relishing every second of it.

"Sounds perfect." Lacing her fingers with his, Violet watched the desert roll past the windows, secure in the notion that 'just in case' wasn't really necessary. She'd packed enough danger into one life already. Nothing in the time to come could touch what they'd lived through.

As they drove, Truck's fingertips dabbled in her palm. Prodding ever so slightly.

Violet's cheeks warmed, and they weren't alone. In short order, the space between her thighs turned into a sex hungry furnace.

"You're bad."

"Am I?" He tickled up her arm, then buried his hand in her hair, alternately rubbing her scalp and taking fistfuls and pulling lightly. "How terrible it must be for you."

"I'll admit," Violet gazed at him with honeyed eyes, "when you said we should do something nice for ourselves, I thought you meant something else."

"Is that right?" His thumb caressed her neck, then rode up the line of her jaw and tipped her chin up. "Such as?"

Violet's lips parted, and she took Truck's thumb into her mouth. Her tongue bathed every bit, sucking it as deep in her throat as she could and raking gently with her teeth.

The rig rumbled along, each vibration in the seat growing

more delectable as her body blossomed to life again. They rolled over a series of bumps, and her core danced with glimmering light. Her mouth fell open in a groan and Truck's thumb slipped out.

"Do that again."

"What?" He grinned, steering towards another patch of uneven pavement. Layla juddered over it, and Violet pressed herself into the seat to feel every pulse. "Is this what you wanted?"

"Yes." Her breath came in short in the *best* way.

"Okay," Truck teased. "I thought you might have something else in mind." As he spoke, he tugged free the button on her trousers. White hot hunger flashed from her core down her legs, her thighs quivering.

She spun in her seat and put her back against the door, spreading her legs so that Truck had full access. He tugged her pants down just enough to pull her panties to the side. Violet was so wet she worried she'd leave a mark on the seat, but once Truck's fingertip brushed her aching slit, everything else evaporated.

"God." Her hand shot out to brace on the dash, and her other gripped the seat like she wanted to rip the stuffing out of it. She rocked her hips forward with a grunt, begging him with her body for more.

Truck answered the call. He delved into her with such confidence her brain dissolved. Each bump in the desert floor sent sparks shooting behind her eyelids. Violet pressed her head against the window so hard it was bound to crack.

Fumbling frantically as she humped Truck's fingers, she found the button and rolled the window down. Wind whistled through her ears, and her hair whipped as she tipped back and let her head hang out the window. Giving over to it, she screamed over and over again into the desert air as Truck guided her to the shimmering star of her climax.

The closer she got, the more insistent his fingers became.

Her breath chased so high in her chest she thought she'd shatter. Just when everything was about to break loose, Truck put Layla on a run of gravel.

Devious, delectable, divine.

Violet grabbed his arm with both hands, arching her back so hard her ass lifted off the seat. A howl of pure pleasure pealed through her, flying up her throat, past her lips, and into the wide open sky.

Each time she thought it couldn't get more intense, they'd hit another bump and she'd go rocketing off again.

"Please," she gasped, trying to pry his arm away. "Stop. Stop. Let me catch my breath."

"Yes, my love." Truck withdrew, and Violet melted into a puddle in the seat. Every inch of her buzzed and glowed like gold. Not just from the cataclysmic orgasm he'd just inflicted upon her.

He called me his love.

Violet's eyelids were heavy, so she figured that's why Truck shone with a glistening aura when she looked at him. His hand rested on her trembling thigh, grazing lightly as the wind played with the tresses hanging out the window.

"Satisfied?" He looked awfully pleased with himself.

"Almost." Her answer startled him so much he actually took his eyes off the plains ahead to look at her. Violet could see the instant it dawned on him what she wanted.

"Hang on, let me put her in park."

"Don't you dare."

Violet slid between the seats, undoing his pants and easing them down until his cock jabbed into the open. It was rigid and ready, and she took it into her mouth eagerly.

"Shit." Truck hissed between his teeth, his hand resting lightly at the base of her neck as she sucked him to the back of her throat. His already improbably swollen cock stiffened further, to the point where she couldn't take all of him.

Pulling back, she ran the tip of her tongue around the

crown and stripped off her pants and underwear. Then she climbed into his seat, straddling him. Truck shied away from her, his whole body tensing.

"We should really stop if we're going to –"

Violet settled over him before he could finish. Protestations weren't her speed at the moment. A girl needs what a girl needs, and this girl *needed it.*

With one glorious thrust he was fully seated, and that familiar sparkle deep within electrified her body. Truck fit perfectly, flooding her with pleasure while nudging just at the underside of pain. Right on the cusp of being too big, he filled her until her cup ranneth right the fuck over.

And over again.

She ground in his lap and clung to his body as Truck charged across the desert and back onto the open road. They really should have cut it out once they were back among the civilized, but *literally* fuck it.

If a cop pulled them over, the poor dickhead would just have to wait until they were done.

And they were gonna take their time.

Violet came over and over again before Truck finally lost himself. When he did, Layla lurched to the side, almost cleaning out a guy changing his tire. The guy screamed like they'd shot his dog, but Violet flashed her tits out the window and that seemed to settle him down.

Just like they planned, they retrieved his trailer, then went back to Dean's compound and took everything that wasn't nailed down. The place was a no-shit buzzard buffet, and Violet supposed the birds would have the whole place cleaned out within a week. In seven days' time, a scrap yard of busted motorcycles would be all that remained of The Pack.

Returning to the room Dean had set aside for them, Truck and Violet took the longest, hottest shower in human history, fucking the entire time.

When they stepped into the open again, the sky was growing dark. An enormous harvest moon hung low and orange in the sky. They stopped to gaze up at it, and she squeezed Truck's hand while she waited.

Nothing.

No hectic anarchy in her blood.

No bone splintering torment as her body reformed itself.

Violet inhaled as deeply as she could. The air was rotten with the stink of death and decay, but to her it was the sweetest breath she'd ever taken.

She was free.

She would never turn into an animal again.

Well, not like that, anyway.

She and Truck would still succumb to their wild sides several times that night.

And every night for a long time to come.

ACKNOWLEDGMENTS

It's astounding to me that this wild, woolly little book is actually hitting the public. Because it's... Not quite regular fare. It's a throwback to all the funky movies I grew up watching, with a bit of extra sugar and spice piled on top.

So, as ever, I have to thank my parents first. John and Kay have fostered this gonzo imagination of mine since I was a little whippersnapper, and their continued love and support is everything.

Next, I gotta give it up to Aimee Ferro, the editor who gets me right down to the bones. My favorite collaborator by a country mile.

Well... Almost.

Big thanks to Dan Hodge and Sharp Levarius over at Trashcan Publishing, as well as Marion Foy for being one of the brightest stars in my little sky. I can't wait to see what happens next!

ABOUT DIDI POUNDER

—"I could never write those books. The pen would catch fire."

Didi Pounder has been a professional ghostwriter since 2019, authoring or co-authoring dozens of novels. Not only is she ready to have her own work out in the open, she thinks it's about damn time.

When not writing, she enjoys taking long walks along the Dalmatian Coast, eating oysters, sipping wine, and living a life she never dreamed of.

— "We only get one shot at this, so why not use both barrels?"

instagram.com/didipounder

www.ingramcontent.com/pod-product-compliance
Lightning Source LLC
Chambersburg PA
CBHW012304011225
36191CB00053B/2177

* 9 7 8 1 9 6 8 3 5 7 0 4 7 *